One Hot
CHRISTMAS

Other Books by Anna Durand

Lachlan in a Kilt (The Ballachulish Trilogy, Book One)
Aidan in a Kilt (The Ballachulish Trilogy, Book Two)
Rory in a Kilt (The Ballachulish Trilogy, Book Three)
The American Wives Club (A Hot Brits/Hot Scots/Au Naturel Crossover)
Brit vs. Scot (A Hot Brits/Hot Scots/Au Naturel Crossover)
Dangerous in a Kilt (Hot Scots, Book One)
Wicked in a Kilt (Hot Scots, Book Two)
Scandalous in a Kilt (Hot Scots, Book Three)
The MacTaggart Brothers Trilogy (Hot Scots, Books 1-3)
Gift-Wrapped in a Kilt (Hot Scots, Book Four)
Notorious in a Kilt (Hot Scots, Book Five)
Insatiable in a Kilt (Hot Scots, Book Six)
Lethal in a Kilt (Hot Scots, Book Seven)
Irresistible in a Kilt (Hot Scots, Book Eight)
Devastating in a Kilt (Hot Scots, Book Nine)
Spellbound in a Kilt (Hot Scots, Book Ten)
Relentless in a Kilt (Hot Scots, Book Eleven)
The Notorious Dr. MacT (A Hot Scots Prequel)
The British Bastard (A Hot Scots Prequel)
One Hot Chance (Hot Brits, Book One)
One Hot Roomie (Hot Brits, Book Two)
One Hot Crush (Hot Brits, Book Three)
The Dixon Brothers Trilogy (Hot Brits, Books 1-3)
One Hot Escape (Hot Brits, Book Four)
One Hot Rumor (Hot Brits, Book Five)
One Hot Scandal (Hot Brits, Book Seven)
Natural Passion (Au Naturel Trilogy, Book One)
Natural Impulse (Au Naturel Trilogy, Book Two)
Natural Satisfaction (Au Naturel Trilogy, Book Three)
Echo Power (Echo Power Trilogy, Book One)
Echo Dominion (Echo Power Trilogy, Book Two)
Echo Unbound (Echo Power Trilogy, Book Three)
The Mortal Falls (Undercover Elementals, Book One)
The Mortal Fires (Undercover Elementals, Book Two)
The Mortal Tempest (Undercover Elementals, Book Three)
The Janusite Trilogy (Undercover Elementals, Books 1-3)
Obsidian Hunger (Undercover Elementals, Book Four)
Unbidden Hunger (Undercover Elementals, Book Five)
The Thirteenth Fae (Undercover Elementals, Book Six)
Willpower (Psychic Crossroads, Book One)
Intuition (Psychic Crossroads, Book Two)
Kinetic (Psychic Crossroads, Book Three)
Passion Never Dies: The Complete Reborn Series

One Hot CHRISTMAS

Hot Brits, Book Six

ANNA DURAND

JACOBSVILLE BOOKS · MARIETTA, OHIO`

ONE HOT CHRISTMAS

ISBN: 978-1-949406-65-8 (paperback)
ISBN: 978-1-949406-66-5 (ebook)
ISBN: 978-1-949406-67-2 (audiobook)

Manufactured in the United States.

Jacobsville Books
www.JacobsvilleBooks.com

Publisher's Cataloging-in-Publication Data
provided by Five Rainbows Cataloging Services

Names: Durand, Anna.
Title: One hot Christmas / Anna Durand.
Description: Marietta, OH : Jacobsville Books, 2021. | Series: Hot Brits, bk. 6.
Identifiers: ISBN 978-1-949406-65-8 (paperback) | ISBN 978-1-949406-66-5 (ebook) | ISBN 978-1-949406-67-2 (audiobook)
Subjects: LCSH: Kings, queens, rulers, etc.--Fiction. | Holidays--Fiction. | Masseurs--Fiction. | New Hampshire--Fiction. | British--Fiction. || Romance fiction. | BISAC: FICTION / Romance / Contemporary. | FICTION / Romance / Romantic Comedy. | FICTION / Romance / Later in Life. | FICTION / Romance / Holiday. | GSAFD: Love stories.
Classification: LCC PS3604.U724 O544 2020 (print) | LCC PS3604.U724 (ebook) | DDC 813/.6--dc23.

Chapter One

Ben

Sometimes a bloke knows when disaster is about to strike, and he prepares for it in whatever way he can, even if it's just to squeeze his eyes shut and brace for impact. This is not one of those times. I had no idea what lay ahead for me until it was too late to do anything other than scream for help.

Uh, scratch that. I didn't say "scream." I said "shout for help in a manly way." I wish I could say I rescued myself from disaster, but I'm not an action hero. I'm a massage therapist.

Maybe I should go back to the beginning.

I had a brilliant life living in England with my mates and working as a massage therapist at a day spa in a little Essex village. I loved it there. Nick Hunter, my boss and my friend, gave me the job despite the fact I'm not a normal employee. He overlooks my past and my family. Nick is amazing, and so is his twin brother Richard. The Dixon brothers have become good mates too. So yeah, I had a perfect life.

Until three months ago, when my mother summoned me home.

No, maybe I shouldn't think about that right now. It's not important to my disaster story, anyway. Let's just say my mother tried to pull me back into the family "business," and after three months of that bollocks, I'd had enough. I plotted my escape, which led me to America—New Hampshire, to be precise. My mate Chance Dixon lives in this state, but he and his wife Elena and their baby daughter have gone off to Switzerland for Christmas. Chance has lent me his house for the holidays. That's where I'm headed, to Chance and Elena's place.

Well, that was the plan. But now I'm lost in a snowstorm.

And of course, the bloody GPS thing on my phone decides now is a good time to snuff it. I try smacking my phone, but that stupid app refuses to resurrect itself. It's dead—and I'll be joining that bloody app soon enough if I can't find my way out of this blizzard. The wind has kicked up, whirling the snow round and round, obscuring my view of the road ahead. Asphalt gave way to gravel a while ago, and I'm starting to worry I've made a wrong turn. The car's headlights can't penetrate the deepening gloom, so it's hard to tell if the sun is setting or if the snow has gotten so thick that it's mimicking twilight.

I see trees. Nothing but trees.

Well, trees and ruddy snow.

Can't get even one bar on my phone, which means I have no hope of ringing for help. Who would I call, anyway? I'm in the middle of sodding nowhere in a country I've never visited before without even a map to guide me. I'd bought a road map, the paper kind, but I managed to cock that up too. It's a map of New Mexico, not New Hampshire.

I squint through the windscreen at the snow. Can't see a thing.

Thump. The right front corner of the car slants down and to the side, and the vehicle won't move even one more inch.

Perfect. Now I've driven into a ditch or a hole. Whichever it is, I'm stuck. The wheels only spin when I press down on the accelerator. Oh, bloody hell. No phone signal, no GPS, no way to tell where I am or to figure out how to get my car unstuck. Should I get out and walk? The snow looks awfully deep, like it might soon pile up higher than the wheels on my car, the one that doesn't belong to me because I hired it at the airport. I brought winter clothes, of course, but not the sort designed for trudging through a blizzard.

"Fuck," I hiss through my clenched teeth. "You're a bloody stupid arse, aren't you, Ben? Yeah, I think I'll drive to Chance's place on my own with a map of New Mexico to guide me, and gee, maybe

I'll get my stupid arse stuck in the snow on a road in the exact middle of nothing. Brilliant plan, mate."

Now I'm chastising myself—out loud. Christ, I've lost my mind.

The wind whips up a whirling dervish of snow that buffets the car, making it shiver. The engine sputters, then quits.

I am going to die out here, aren't I? They'll find my frozen remains in the spring, crumpled over the steering wheel.

A flash of light up ahead jerks me out of my miserable fantasy of Ben the Ice Mummy. What was that flash? Maybe I imagined it. Another burst of light pierces the falling snow. No, I did not imagine that. A one-eyed vehicle of some sort is barreling toward me. Straight toward me. On a head-on collision trajectory. Since my car decided to die on me, that means the headlights went out too. The person or persons in that one-eyed vehicle can't see me.

Bugger. I'm about to get creamed by…whatever that thing is.

I try to open the driver's door, but it won't budge. I shove and shove, throwing my whole body into it, but the door refuses to open. Doesn't that just figure? I finally escape from my mother's clutches, only to die when a motorized Cyclops crashes into my car.

The light slows down and stops bobbing. It remains stationary several yards ahead of my car, but I still can't make out what the vehicle is. A figure emerges from the swirling snow—a figure dressed all in pink, including a pink helmet. A woman? Maybe it's a bloke who likes pink. I don't care who it is as long as they can get me out of this bloody car and to a warm, safe place.

The figure stops beside the driver's door and knocks on the glass.

I can't roll down the window. It's electric, and the car is dead. So I raise my hands and shrug, shouting, "It won't open."

My savior nods, then disappears into the blizzard again. The pink person comes back a moment later carrying a small shovel. It only takes a minute to clear the snow away from the car door, then the mystery man or woman pulls it open and waves for me to get out.

I grab my parka from the backseat and clamber out.

And trip over a rock or something that's hidden in the snow, falling flat on my face in the damn white stuff. Snow is very cold. More so than I expected. And it's melting in my nose. Small but strong hands push under my arms and hoist me out of the snow, onto my knees. The wind buffets me, cold and sharp, suddenly making me wish I'd brought a ski mask. I clamber to my feet and do my best to brush off the snow. Some of it has already melted and made my trousers damp.

My savior pushes up the face shield on that pink helmet, and I get my first glimpse of the person who rescued me. I see lovely green eyes with thick, dark lashes, as well as an adorable nose that turns up slightly at the end. My gaze travels down to the mystery person's chest.

This is definitely a girl. Not many blokes have such nice, round breasts.

I open my mouth to thank the angel, but she speaks first.

"We can chitchat later," she says. "Better take you to a warm place before you get frostbite. Did you bring any serious winter clothing?"

"Isn't this serious?" I ask, gesturing at the parka I've just pulled on.

We both need to almost shout to hear each other over the wind and the creaking of the trees. I can't help picturing an enormous branch snapping off one of those trees to slam down on my head. That would just be my luck.

I have started to shiver a bit, so this girl might have a point about getting to a warm place.

She waves for me to follow as she trots back to her snowmobile. Yes, I can now see that's what the machine is. I hurry after the girl as fast as I can, but the snow is at least two feet deep here. Can't understand how the woman who rescued me can slog through this mess like it's candyfloss, but I'm getting winded and starting to sweat. When I reach the snowmobile, a black one with pink accent stripes, she hands me a full-face helmet almost identical to hers.

A black helmet, thankfully. Pink isn't my color.

The girl climbs astride the machine and pushes down the face shield on her helmet.

I climb on behind her.

She glances back at me. "Better hold on to me. It'll be a bumpy ride."

"All right." I feel a bit weird about it, but I wrap my arms around her waist. I've never hugged a stranger so tightly before, but she did mention a bumpy ride ahead. "I'm ready."

The snowmobile revs up, and we're off.

As my new mate drives past my car, she calls out, "We'll come back for your stuff in the morning. Okay?"

"Sure."

The girl finds a wider spot in the road and turns around, then seems to hit the accelerator, or whatever machines like this one have, and we rocket away. I cling to her as the forest streaks by, my teeth clacking every time we bounce over a lump on the ground or…I don't know what. Can't really see, what with a blizzard raging around us and my helmet obscuring my view. Soon, I notice lights up ahead. They don't look like vehicle headlights, so maybe that's a house I see. My assumption is confirmed when we stop in the driveway of a modest-size log cabin, near the porch steps.

My savior angel shuts off the snowmobile's engine. "Let's get inside."

I dismount from the machine a bit more clumsily than I would've liked. A pretty girl saved me, and now I'm bumbling around like I'm on drugs. I'm not, I swear. But our ride through the woods has left me feeling slightly off balance.

Still, I manage to follow the girl into the cabin.

As she shuts the door behind us, every muscle in my body relaxes for the first time in at least an hour, maybe longer. I got lost, then got bogged down in a blizzard, and then my car died… Yeah, I've had some stress. We take off our helmets, and I finally see all of her face.

This girl is beautiful. Her long blonde hair falls over her shoulders now, though it seems to have been tucked up inside her helmet before. It still looks a little squashed. Since I know she has dark lashes and dark eyebrows, I assume she's not a natural blonde, but I don't care.

She pushes her hands into her hair and shakes her head while she combs her locks out with her fingers. A smile curves her luscious mouth. "Ahhh, much better."

The girl reaches out to remove my helmet.

Why? Because I've been standing here like a bloody statue, gawping at the pretty girl who saved my life. What a brilliant first impression I'm making.

"How are you feeling?" she asks.

"Not bad, considering I almost died out there."

"Glad you didn't." She taps the tip of my nose. "A cutie like you shouldn't become a human Popsicle."

She thinks I'm cute? I definitely think she's adorable.

I glance at my surroundings, taking note of a large fireplace behind us that has flames dancing away. The room also has a sofa, two armchairs, a coffee table, and some other smaller pieces of furniture that seem more decorative than practical. A Christmas tree stands in one corner, its multicolored lights brightening the space, while red, green, and gold garlands decorate the walls and the island in the open kitchen.

As I peel off my parka, I notice seven stockings hanging from the mantel. Does she have family staying here too? A husband and kids?

"Oh no," she coos in a sympathetic tone while she studies my clothing. "You're all wet, aren't you? Poor baby. You get those soppy clothes off while I find some dry stuff for you to wear. There's a blanket on the sofa that you can wrap yourself in while I get clothes for you."

She turns away, hurrying toward a hallway. I see a staircase to the left of the front door, but she breezes right past it.

I clear my throat. "Is there, ah, anyone else here?"

"Nope. Just us." She flashes me a grin over her shoulder. "Afraid I'll attack you while you sleep? I might do that, but only if you want me to."

She's flirting with me, isn't she?

Maybe my holiday started out as a disaster, but things are looking up now.

Chapter Two

Sam

Did I just flirt with a stranger I picked up on the road? Sure, I enjoy flirting with guys. But I don't even know his name. I couldn't help myself, though. He is a total cutie-pie, and I love his British accent. While I try to avoid thinking about the anonymous man in my living room, I search for something my guest can wear. Mostly, I've got women's clothing because I am a woman, after all. Digging around in the walk-in closet in my bedroom, I discover an old box that has some clothes in it. Men's clothes. Don't think the sizes are quite right for the cutie-pie in the living room, but it'll have to do.

With a bundle of clothes in my arms, I head back out there.

And I freeze just past the end of the hall, alongside the stairs to the second floor.

My guest is standing in front of the fire, naked. I mean one hundred percent naked. Since he's facing away from me, I get a spectacular view of his backside and his taut ass. This guy has muscles, though not the bulging, super-ripped kind. No, he has the body of a man who cares about staying in shape but isn't obsessed with exercising. I can't stop my gaze from exploring every inch of him, from his muscular shoulders down to his toned thighs. I bet he's got stamina in the bedroom.

Why am I thinking about sex? He's a stranger.

He turns around, his eyes closed and a soft smile on his lips. The heat of the fire must feel fantastic to inspire an expression like that.

And wow, I can see everything. He has a great chest, but it's the area between his hips that captures my attention and refuses to let me look away. His dick hangs slack, but I can tell it will be long and sleek when he gets aroused. Not a single vein mars that perfect cock. I might be starting to drool, but I don't care. No woman could stop herself from salivating over a man who has that kind of beautiful body. I love his face too, of course. He's adorable, with those blue eyes that I saw earlier and that slightly crooked nose, not to mention lips that are neither too small nor too big, just right for kissing.

But oh, that dick. I'm getting tingly all over just looking at it.

My hold on the clothes in my arms falters, and a few items flop onto the floor.

The naked cutie's eyes pop open, then flare wide. He shields his privates with his hands, glancing around as if he's searching for something. "Ah, sorry. I didn't think you'd be back so soon, and I was cold, so I—" He grimaces. "Sorry. The fire felt good."

Damn, it's endearing how he keeps saying "sorry" while blushing.

"Oh, don't worry about it. I've seen naked men before." My cheeks have started to feel warm, and so have other parts of me. I snag the clothes that I'd dropped and hustle over to the sofa to drop all the items on the cushions. "Here you go. Should be something in this bundle that you can wear. I'll go make some hot cocoa. Or would you prefer tea?"

"Whatever you're having is fine with me."

"Okay. Back in a jiff."

I force myself to walk at a normal pace as I enter the open kitchen, which has only a bar separating it from the living room. My guest seems embarrassed by his full frontal and rear exposure, so pretending I didn't notice his hot bod or his gorgeous manly bits seems like the best way to handle the situation. I love his hair too, the way it's the same color as milk chocolate. Or maybe it's more like wet beach sand, which is darker than the dry version.

Wet. I shouldn't have thought that word, because now I'm dreaming up some naughty fantasies involving water.

Get a grip, girl. Chastising myself doesn't help, but focusing on the task at hand does. I get the cocoa powder out of the cupboard, grab the sugar bowl, and bring out a carton of milk. Ooh, I need vanilla too. Cocoa tastes even yummier that way. While I toss ingredients into two mugs, I keep my back to the living room. I can hear that sexy cutie-pie getting dressed, thanks to the rustling sounds his clothes make.

I've just dropped marshmallows into the cocoa when the hottie in the living room speaks.

"All good now," he says. "Safe to turn around."

With a mug in each hand, I turn around and march back into the living room.

He's wearing a purple and blue sweater that drapes over his torso like it was designed for a sumo wrestler. His pants, on the other hand, seem one size too small. I don't mind the way the blue jeans cling to his legs and accentuate the bulge of his cock. No, I don't mind that at all. But I can only see that bulge when he lifts the hem of the sweater to pooch it out to show me how overly large it is.

"I think you and I could both fit in this," he says, "and invite several of our mates to join us."

Snuggling up inside that sweater with him sounds way too good. I mean, I don't even know his name. But I can fix that problem.

I give him a mug of cocoa, then hold out my now-free hand. "Think we should introduce ourselves. I'm Samantha Lockhart, but everybody calls me Sam."

"Bennett Montague," he says, while slipping his palm into mine. "It's a pleasure to meet you. May I call you Sam? You can call me Ben. I prefer that."

"Sure, Ben, you can call me Sam." He can call me anything he wants as long as he says it in that accent. "Sorry about the sweater. The only men's clothing I could find were things that belonged to my grandfather. He was a large man, but he had skinny legs."

"He *was* large?"

"Yeah. Grandpa passed away two years ago."

"Oh, I'm sorry to hear that. Did you two get on well?"

I take a sip of my cocoa, letting the chocolatey goodness glide over my tongue and ooze warmth down my throat. "We were very close. He left me this cabin because I always loved visiting him here."

"Sounds like you have a lot of good memories of him."

"Mm-hm." I take another sip, then glance at his mug. "Are you going to drink that? It'll warm you up on the inside. Besides, I slaved away over a hot microwave to whip that up."

"Sorry." He takes a swig of his cocoa. "Mm, that's delicious. Best I've ever had."

"No need to lay it on so thick. I don't mind if my cocoa isn't the most wonderful on earth."

"But I'm not laying it on thick. I'm serious." He drinks some more and smiles. "Definitely the best I've ever had."

Oh, he could absolutely be the best I've ever had. I have a sixth sense about these things. Lustful psychic flashes are my specialty.

"Why don't we sit down?" I say.

"Sure."

I settle onto the sofa, but he takes one of the armchairs. Damn. I'd hoped he might sit next to me just so I can smell him. I bet he smells good. Lust at first sight isn't my thing, honestly. Dating, getting to know a guy, that's the right way to lead up to sex. Pulling a man out of a snowdrift and bringing him back to my place, where he strips naked for me, is not my usual method of getting laid.

Not that I plan on doing that with Ben. I don't do casual sex.

But he's so cute and hot. I could nibble on him for hours.

Weren't you supposed to be getting a grip, girl? Snap to it.

"So, where are you from, Ben?" I ask.

He fidgets in his chair, his whole face crimped. "That's a complicated question."

"Really? I always thought it was an easy question. Do you have amnesia and can't remember where you live?"

"No, that's not the issue." He guzzles his cocoa, then coughs several times. "Sorry. I drank too fast."

I smile. "Yeah, you kind of did. It's cocoa, not booze."

"Yes, I know." He sets his mug down on the little table beside his chair. "And I remember where I live. It's a village called Cockshire, in southeast England. I work there too, at a day spa owned by a mate."

"Mate means friend, right? Here in America, it usually means a significant other or maybe a prisoner in a jail cell. Oh wait, those are *in*mates, right? Not just mates."

"It's a good thing you're so adorable or I might be offended by that joke." He grins. "Actually, no, I wouldn't. I'm not that sensitive."

Did he just call me adorable? And he's smiling at me with a twinkle in his eyes. I could eat him up, that's how cuddly hot he is. Yes, a man can be both snuggly-wuggly and smokin' hot. Ben Montague proves that point.

"What about you?" he asks. "Where do you work and live?"

"I live here. There's a town about ten miles away. I do my shopping there, unless I need something special. Then I order online."

"And what about work?"

"Do that here too, at home. I'm a virtual assistant." He looks vaguely confused, as people often do when I tell them what line of work I'm in, so I explain. "That means people hire me to help them arrange their work schedules, remind them of appointments, do research for them, invoice their clients, basically anything that makes it easier for them to do their jobs."

"Ah, I see. Sounds like interesting work."

"Can be." I tuck my feet under me cross-legged while I sip my cocoa. "You said you work at a day spa. What exactly do you do there?"

"I'm a massage therapist. Mostly, I work with clients who are injured or elderly."

"You must be good with your hands." And yes, I'm imagining his hands rubbing me down. Can't help it. He's gorgeous and sweet, and I haven't been with anyone in months.

But no, I will not sleep with him. We just met, for heaven's sake.

My resolve lasts for exactly eight seconds, according to the mantel clock. Then he announces, "I'd be happy to give you a free massage as thanks for saving my life."

Oh yeah, now I desperately want him to touch me all over.

"That's a sweet offer," I say, "but it's late, and we should both get some rest. The sofa pulls out into a bed. Are you okay with sleeping out here? This cabin only has one bedroom. Well, technically two. But I'm using the upstairs room for storage."

"No worries. I can camp out by the fire."

"I'll get you pillows and a blanket. The sheets are already on the bed."

We both get up, and Ben helps me pull out the sofa bed. Then I rush back to my room to grab those pillows and a blanket for my guest. I haven't hosted any guests since I started living here, and it's kind of nice to have some company. I also grab a robe in case he wants that. I don't have any pajamas for him to sleep in, not even a pair of boxers. A robe will have to suffice.

I sleep in a teddy, but I can't give him one of those to wear. He's much bigger than I am.

Though I try to put the blanket on the sofa bed, my guest refuses to let me help him with that task. He shoos me away with a smile. How can I argue with such a sweet hottie? I say good night and go back to my room.

Though I try to sleep, I can't stop thinking about Ben. The fact that I'd seen him in the buff does nothing to temper my lust for that man. I shouldn't think about his job, because that leads to fantasies of his hands all over my body, but my mind has other ideas. It treats me to vivid images of Ben massaging me from head to toe and giving me a happy ending with those fingers and that mouth. I can't explain why I want a man I just met. It's never happened to me before. But there's something about him that makes me completely nuts in the sexiest way imaginable.

I need to relieve this damp ache between my thighs. Need to do it so badly. But I have a guest who's sleeping twenty feet away from my bedroom. What if he heard me getting off? I've never been good at staying quiet either during sex or when I make myself come. So no, I will not do that. Just have to live with the lust until I finally get sleepy.

An hour after I crawled under my sheets, I develop a strong need to pee. So I slink out of my room, aiming for the bathroom across the hall. I bump into Ben. Literally. We crash into each other in the semi-dark, with only the muted glow from the hall night-light to dispel the shadows. I should move away from him, but I can't convince my muscles to move.

Ben is naked.

Sheesh, I gave him a robe, for pity's sake. Why isn't he wearing it?

"Did I scare you?" he asks in that sinfully sexy British accent.

"No, not scared."

"Good." He lashes an arm around me. "I want to kiss you, Sam."

Oh God, yes, I want that. But all I can manage to say is, "Okay."

He grips my bottom in both hands and lifts me to level our faces—and then he kisses me.

Chapter Three

Ben

I'm kissing Sam. *Kissing* her. The woman I met a few hours ago just agreed to let me glue my mouth to hers and thrust my tongue between those sexy lips. She tastes like mint. Toothpaste, I assume. Don't care because it feels so bloody good to have her lips molded to mine and her tongue teasing me, not to mention her tits pasted to my chest with their stiff tips poking me. Every ounce of blood in my body seems to have flooded down to my cock, hardening it in record time. I don't want to stop with a kiss. I want to drag her down to the floor and shag her right this instant.

But I'm not the sort to do that. It wouldn't be right.

I want to do it, though. Didn't I run away to New Hampshire because I needed to escape from my life? Can't think of a better way to do that than to fuck the sexy girl who rescued me from a blizzard. Maybe this is a strange type of post-traumatic stress. But I didn't feel all that traumatized by my experience on the road, not once Sam found me.

Christ, her arse is perfect. I love cradling it in my hands, but I love it even more when I massage those cheeks and she moans into my mouth.

And now I'm swerving back to my original plan—shag her right here, right now. Well, not literally right here. The wood floor is too hard. So I sweep her up in my arms and carry her into the living room.

Maybe I wouldn't be doing this if I didn't know I'd be leaving tomorrow, as soon as the blizzard winds down and the road is cleared. That can't take too long, can it? Suddenly, I don't care if I'm stuck in this cabin for a month. But the knowledge that I will most likely leave tomorrow drives me to do this tonight, with her. I need to feel her body wrapped around me once before we say goodbye.

I lay her down on the sofa bed. It's surprisingly soft, with just enough bounce. While I keep kissing Sam, I yank her satin shorts down to her ankles, and she kicks them off. Then I whisk the satin top off over her head. Only then do I take a moment to admire the woman lying beneath me on the sofa bed, while I kneel at her feet. She has the most beautiful body I've ever seen, from her small, round breasts with their dusky nipples down to her flat belly and her toned thighs. But my attention keeps veering back to her hips and the curly hairs that already glisten with droplets of her cream. I need to gorge myself on her for hours, but honestly, I don't think I can last that long, not when I want her this badly.

"Please, Ben," she says, and spreads her thighs. "I want your mouth on me first."

I want that too. So I lower myself onto the bed with my face between her legs and push my mouth into her slick folds. The aroma of her intoxicates me, and I almost feel drunk as I devour her clit, licking and sucking while she gasps and arches her hips. Sam tastes so bloody wonderful that I never want to stop, but I need to make her come for me. I drag my tongue down one side of her folds and back up the other side, then I latch on to her nub again and suckle it while I plunge a finger into her core.

She grips the pillow in both hands, her eyes squeezed shut but her mouth open like she wants to cry out but can't.

I slide two fingers inside her, thrusting hard and fast while curling my fingers to pet the silky flesh of her inner wall. Faster and faster I thrust, pinching her clit between my teeth.

"Ben!" she cries out as her entire body goes rigid.

I keep devouring her until the muscles inside her body stop clenching my fingers.

"More," she whispers. "Don't stop yet. I need you inside me."

Just as I kneel over her, gazing down at her face, I realize something and groan. "Fuck, I don't have a condom."

The girl I need to shag like mad makes a pained face. "I was on the pill, but I stopped taking it when I decided not to date for a while."

I drop onto the bed on my back, sprawled beside her. No sex for me tonight.

Sam sits up and swings one leg over me, straddling my hips. She rests her arse on my thighs. "We can still have sex. Just pull out right before you come."

"Not sure I have the willpower to do that."

"Let me handle that part." She closes her hand around my cock. "I've got willpower."

Does she? Not sure I should trust her self-control since I can't trust mine. But I feel like my cock will explode if I don't fuck her, so… No, I can't do it. If neither of us remembers that I need to pull out before I come, we could be in serious trouble.

Sam decides for me. She rises to her knees and sinks that lush body onto my erection until I'm seated deep inside her. Then she starts to move, rising off me only to sink back down, resting her palms on my chest so she can roll her hips into me, her breaths gasping out of her while the slippery feel of her body cradling my length makes me breathe harder too. She rides me faster, slamming down on me with a wet slapping sound while her cream dribbles onto my thighs. I grasp her hips and buck mine up to meet her thrusts, driving even deeper into her body.

"Fuck," I growl. "I'm about to—"

She pulls out, squatting on my thighs, and pumps me with her hand.

And I come, liquid jetting out of me and onto her belly. She leans back and keeps pumping me until I'm done and her flesh is glistening where I came all over her creamy skin.

"Sorry," I say. "Better wash that off before it dries."

"You can help me wash it off." She leans over to kiss me, sliding her tongue around mine in a slow and deeply sensual way that makes my cock twitch like it might just revive faster than seems humanly possible. "Let's take a shower together."

"Shower? I'll definitely shag you again if we do that."

"I know ways we can do that without risking anything."

No, I shouldn't do what she's suggesting. Maybe her willpower held up this time, but I can't expect her to do that again. I want her even more now. Even knowing I can't come inside her, I need to feel her body clenching me again.

You can't do it, you moron.

"We shouldn't," I say. "This was incredible, but we can't risk it again. Sorry."

"That's okay." She climbs off the bed, grabbing her shorts and top. "I loved being with you, Ben. Glad you got stranded."

"Me too."

She sashays back down the hallway, veering into the bathroom. A few minutes later, I hear her go into her bedroom.

And I just lie here on the sofa bed, gazing up at the ceiling and wondering what just happened. I sort of had sex with a girl I just met. This day has been insane, so I can't be entirely sure I haven't dreamed the whole thing. Samantha Lockhart can't be real. No girl has ever done anything like that with me. I mean, I can't get a leg over with any woman unless I bring out a condom so they can see it and watch me put it on to be sure I won't do anything sneaky. Yeah, the women I've dated have been paranoid, but I overlooked that as being the fault of all those wankers who don't care about the girls they shag. They just want to get off.

Sam and I had done that all right. But I want more.

Maybe that town she mentioned has a store where I can buy condoms.

No, I should leave as soon as possible and get my arse to Chance's house. Everything that happened tonight will become a strange and wonderful memory. I know I can't hide out at Chance's forever because my mother will track me down eventually and abduct me back to Mithoria for another round of "who wants to marry a crown prince."

Bugger me.

I pull the covers over myself—all the way over, with my face under the sheet—and try not to think about anything.

Except for Samantha Lockhart.

Chapter Four

Sam

I wake up the next morning feeling fantastic. Why? Having sex with a stranger shouldn't leave me invigorated, but it does. We only halfway had sex, I suppose, but it still felt incredible. Ben is so damn hot, and he rocks oral sex. I'd love to find out how good he is at the full-on version, but I know he must have someplace to be since he doesn't live in this area. He said he lives in England, though he was cagey about that last night. He didn't dress for backwoods adventure either, which explains how he got all soppy after falling into a snowdrift. I get the impression he has no idea what winter is like in New Hampshire.

Maybe he's never seen snow before. Do they get much of that in England?

After rising and shining, I amble into the living room. Ben has already stowed away the sofa bed, but I don't see him until I reach the kitchen. He's standing on the other side of the bar doing something on the stove. Is he cooking breakfast? None of the men I've dated ever did that. Their idea of making breakfast is to hand me a toaster pastry or a slice of cold pizza.

"Good morning," I say as I approach the bar.

Ben smiles at me over his shoulder. "Good morning. Hope you like sausage, eggs, and toast. I wanted to make you a full English breakfast, but you don't seem to have any baked beans, bacon, or tomatoes."

"That's okay. What you're making smells yummy." I hop onto a stool and study him while he focuses on the frying pan, stirring the food. "Do you seriously eat all that for breakfast? Sounds like a lot of food."

"Not every day. But I enjoy a good full English now and then."

"Don't think Americans have a universal meal. We all do our own thing. My grandfather used to love steak and eggs, but that's way too much for me to eat in the morning."

He glances at me, smiling again, and it's the cutest expression. "Sounds like your grandfather would've fit right in with my family." He nods toward the counter to his left. "I made coffee. Couldn't find any tea."

"So you Brits honestly do love your tea, hey?"

"Yes. Though my mother prefers black coffee in the morning."

I guess we've decided to talk about food to avoid the topic of what we did last night. Sooner or later, though, we'll have to discuss it. Like adults. Calmly and rationally. But I don't feel rational at all when I'm within kissing distance of Ben Montague.

The sunrise shines through the picture window in the living room, painting everything in shades of pink and gold. The blizzard has ended, for sure, which means Ben will leave soon. Can't decide how I feel about that.

"Where are you headed?" I ask. "Assuming the roads are clear."

"A little town called Hartmoor. My mate Chance and his wife have lent me their house for the holidays. They've gone off to Switzerland."

"I've never been to Hartmoor, but I hear it's beautiful up there. Must be about thirty miles to the northwest."

Ben twists his mouth into the most endearing expression of disgust—aimed at himself, I think. "I cocked it up thoroughly, didn't I? Thirty miles off course? Good thing you found me, or I'd have died of frostbite."

"Glad I could be there to rescue you."

"You are my hero, Sam."

I have no idea what to say in response. Nobody has ever called me their hero before, but I can tell Ben means it. He's not being sarcastic or expressing frustration with the fact he needed rescuing. He doesn't seem to mind at all that a woman saved him.

"While you finish whipping up breakfast," I say, "I'll call the county barn to find out if the roads have been plowed yet."

"Sounds like a plan."

I grab my cell phone and dial the number for the county barn. Wayne Hendley answers right away.

"Hi, it's Samantha Lockhart," I say. "Is the road plowed yet? Somebody got bogged down yesterday, and I had to bring him to my place for the night. But I'm sure he wants to get back on the road as soon as possible."

"No can do. I'm afraid the plow's broken down, and it might be tomorrow before it's fixed."

"Oh no, that's terrible." Though I say that, I feel a thrill shivering over my skin. Maybe I want Ben to hang around a little longer, but that's crazy. I barely know him. "My friend had to leave his luggage in his car. Guess I'd better go retrieve it for him."

"I can fetch it for ya. Besides, you don't have a sled to carry the luggage."

"Okay, if you're sure. I don't want to cause you too much trouble."

"No trouble at all. I need to head out that way to check on some of the older folks, anyway."

"Thank you, Wayne. I appreciate your help."

"Sure thing."

We say goodbye, and I turn back to Ben. He's watching me with his brows furrowed while he holds a plate of food in each hand.

"The snowplow broke down," I tell him. "We're stranded here for a while longer. Hopefully, you'll be able to get on your way again tomorrow."

"Oh." He sets the plates down on the bar, on my side. "Sorry to be such a bother."

"You're no bother. It's nice to have some company."

"But you must have work to do." He grabs two mugs of coffee and comes around the bar, perching on the stool beside mine. He hands me a mug. "I don't want you to feel like you need to entertain me."

"No work. I'm taking two weeks off for Christmas." I sip the coffee, which tastes so good this morning. Maybe Ben has a secret coffee recipe, or maybe I just like knowing he'll be here for at least another day. The company of a hot sweetie like him could make the air taste better. "I'm sorry you won't get to spend Christmas in Hartmoor like you planned."

"I'm not sorry." He skims his gaze over me from head to toe. "Starting to like it here."

Why do I get tingly all over when he says that and when he looks at me that way? Oh, who cares why. Ben makes me feel things I haven't felt in a long time. Maybe I've never experienced this kind of attraction before. Instant lust isn't my thing, and I absolutely do not believe in love at first sight. But whatever this is between us, I'd like to keep feeling it for a bit longer.

"Forgot to tell you," I say. "Wayne, the man who runs the county barn, said he'll pick up your luggage and bring it here. He's got a more powerful snowmobile than I do, so he can tow a sled behind it."

Ben glances down at the baggy purple sweater he's wearing. "It would be nice to have my own clothes."

"That reminds me. The outfit you had on last night should be dry now."

"We can get that later. I'm starving."

"Me too."

We dig into our food but don't talk while we're chowing down. I didn't realize how hungry I was until I started eating, and Ben seems like he wasn't exaggerating when he said he was starving. Of course, neither of us ate anything last night. We had sex and went to sleep.

After we've finished our meal, I literally have to pull Ben away from the sink and order him not to do the dishes. He's a guest, for heaven's sake. Besides, he almost froze to death last night. When I say that to him, he laughs.

"A slight exaggeration," he says. "But I surrender. You can do the dishes."

"Thank you."

While he trots off to the laundry room to get his clothes, I start cleaning up. I've washed one plate when someone knocks on the front door. I wipe my hands dry on my jeans as I hurry to open the door.

"Mornin', Sammy," Wayne Hendley says with a big smile. "Hope you and your guest stayed warm last night. It was a chilly one, hey?"

Only Wayne ever calls me Sammy. I'm not crazy about the nickname, but he's such a nice man that I don't want to offend him by announcing I don't like being called that.

"Yeah, it was cold," I say. "But the snow was insane."

"Sure was." He hooks a thumb over his shoulder. "Got your friend's bags in the sled. I'll bring 'em on in."

"Let me help you."

"Nah." He waves a dismissive hand. "You don't even have shoes on. Let me take care of it."

"Thanks, Wayne. You're a lifesaver."

His attention veers to something past my shoulder. "Got your bags for ya. Bring 'em in right now."

Wayne jogs back to his snowmobile, which is parked near the porch steps.

I shut the door and turn around, face to face with Ben. An entire day with the British hottie? Oh, this might be a worse disaster than what happened to Ben last night on the road.

Can my willpower survive spending more time with him?

Chapter Five

Ben

While Sam stares blankly at me like she's gone catatonic, I raise my brows. "Who was that?"

"Huh? Oh, that was Wayne Hendley. He's in charge of the county barn and the snowplow crew."

"I thought they only had one plow, and it's broken."

"True. But whoever's available takes the job of plowing whenever snow hits."

"Makes sense."

At least I'm now wearing my own clothes, the outfit from last night that had gotten soaked during the Great Blizzard Catastrophe. Maybe it wasn't a catastrophe to anyone else, but I will always view it that way. My khaki pants and grey cable-knit sweater will make a better impression than Sam's grandfather's old clothes. I've got my snow boots too.

"That's definitely more your color," Sam says with a teasing smile as she eyes me up and down. "Purple makes you look sallow."

"It makes me look ruddy ridiculous." I pat my thigh. "Flannel-lined trousers. I was ready for the cold, but not for a bloody snowstorm."

"Didn't watch the weather report before you took off on your getaway?"

Though I try not to, I flinch the tiniest bit. "No, I didn't check anything. Just hired a car at the airport and took off."

"What was the big rush?"

"I, ah…" Hunching my shoulders, I jam my hands in my trouser pockets. "I needed to escape from my life for a while. Needed it badly."

"Don't you like your job?"

I wince. How can I explain without telling her everything? The Dixons and the Hunters have always known who I am, and they've always treated me like just another mate, not a sodding crown prince. The few times I told someone else about me, it did not end well. So I tell Sam, "I love my job. It's…other things that aren't working for me."

I can't blame Sam for quizzing me like this. She seems to have an insatiable curiosity, something I can identify with and that I find so endearing that I want to kiss her again. More than anything, I want to ask her questions and learn more about her. But that's a bad idea. The more I know, the more I'll like her. It's inevitable because she is so adorable.

But I stumbled into her life last night, seduced her on the sofa bed a few hours later, and made her breakfast this morning. That's the sum total of our acquaintance so far. I shouldn't let it go any further.

Well, at least Mum isn't likely to track me down here. It seems like the middle of absolutely nowhere.

A fist raps on the front door.

Sam gives up on interrogating me and swings the door open for the man I'd seen a few minutes ago. What did she say his name was? I got distracted by her smile and her sexy body, and the information flew out of my ear. The bloke lugs my suitcases into the living room and sets them down.

"There ya go," he says with a smile. Then he offers his hand to me. "Wayne Hendley. Glad to meet you, mister…"

"Ben Montague," I say, shaking Wayne's hand. "But there's no need to be formal about. Just call me Ben."

"Are you British or something?"

"Yes, I am."

He grins. "Wait'll I tell my wife I met an honest-to-goodness British guy. She'll be tickled pink."

"I'm chuffed to meet another American. Sam's the only one I've talked to since I arrived in New Hampshire."

"Everybody's real nice up here. You'll love it." Wayne slaps my arm. "Once the road's clear, you should stop by my place for dinner before you head out to wherever you're going. My wife cooks the best lobster stew you'll ever eat."

"Isn't this a landlocked state?"

"No," he says with what sounds like sarcastic offense. "We've got a whole eighteen miles of Atlantic shoreline."

"Do you? That's impressive."

"At least we're not stuck in the middle of the North Atlantic like you Brits. You're practically in Greenland." He smirks and waggles his eyebrows. I have no idea what that means, but he returns to normal conversation so I don't get a chance to ask him how the UK is practically in Greenland. "We've got a great little grocery store in town. They get seafood shipped in from Maine, mostly."

"I see. Lobster stew sounds lovely." I say that to be polite, but I'm not at all convinced I want to eat that food. "I'm on my way to Hartmoor, but I got lost."

"Not a backwoods boy, hey? While you're here, you should take a little trip down the hill to North Slipperton. That's the nearest town."

"Is there a South Slipperton?"

"Nope. You'd think there would be, but we've only got North Slipperton. No east or west either."

Sam shuffles closer to us. "But I thought the road was still closed."

"Pete Messing says the trail through his property is in good shape," Wayne tells her. "You should be able to get down the hill no problem. Assuming Ben here can handle the ride. Do you British folks have snowmobiles?"

"I've never seen one," I say. "But then, I don't go to the places where people might need them."

"City boy, eh?"

"No. I just prefer to stay close to home."

"I get it." Wayne sighs, hooking his thumbs inside his waistband. "I'll leave you youngsters to enjoy the day on your own. If you make it into town, get Sam to show you the Crab Cottage. They've got the best seafood for fifty miles." He winks at me. "The Crab Cottage is a restaurant, by the way, not a hotel for crustaceans."

Yes, if he hadn't told me that I would've expected to find lobsters and crabs enjoying afternoon tea at the cottage.

Wayne ambles out of the house, shutting the door.

I hunch my shoulders. "Should we go into the village?"

"Sure, if you want. Supposed to be warmer today, so you won't freeze riding on my machine."

"The pink-striped snowmobile."

"Yep. You got a problem with riding on a pink-striped machine?"

"No. I think my manly pride can handle it."

"Good. Let's go into town, hey?"

Sam pulls on her snowsuit and boots while I grab my parka and gloves. I wasn't prepared for a blizzard, but I did bring warm clothes. Not the sort for a snow emergency and a wild ride on a pink beast, though. Maybe I can correct that mistake.

As we're walking out the door, I ask, "Is there a shop in town where I can buy a suit like yours? In a different color, of course."

"Sure. We'll stop in at the Discount Depot."

The woman I halfway shagged last night puts on her helmet and mounts the pink-striped beast. I slip on the black helmet I'd worn last night and wrap my arms around Sam's waist. There's something slightly erotic about sitting astride a grumbling, vibrating machine while hugging a sexy woman. What we did last night doesn't help matters. So I focus on the scenery as we roar down the "hill," as Wayne had called it, though this seems more like a mountain to me. Sam weaves around trees with ease, and she seems to be taking it a bit slower than last night, probably because I'm not in danger of dying from frostbite today. The sun shines down on us as we zoom closer and closer to the village I can now see below us.

North Slipperton, here I come.

Once we get into town, Sam pulls up behind a boxy building and parks the snowmobile behind it. The building has grey shingles all over it. I suppose there's a technical term for that sort of siding or whatever they call it, but I've never had much interest in architecture. I'm much more concerned with the female anatomy at the moment.

Sam wriggles her arse, rubbing it against my cock, then slides off the seat. When she pulls her helmet off, she thrusts her fingers into her hair to fluff it up, since it got plastered to her skull.

I desperately need to shag her—properly this time. Maybe the shop she mentioned carries condoms.

Sam leads me to the front of the building, and I see the sign on the front, high above us on the second story. It says, "Discount Depot, North Slipperton's Favorite Clothing & Hardware Store."

"Are there a lot of clothing and hardware stores in this town?" I ask.

"No," Sam says with a slight chuckle. "This one's all we have. So naturally, it's everyone's favorite. That's New England humor for you."

"Americans are very strange, but I think of it as charming rather than a sign of insanity."

She rolls her eyes. "A nation that eats blood sausage shouldn't look down their noses at New England ways."

"I hate blood sausage."

"You do?" She gives me a look of fake shock. "Are you sure you're British?"

"I was born in England, so yes, I am British."

But I'm also Mithorian. I do not want to explain my dual citizenship to Sam, not now, probably not ever. She'd want to know more about my homeland, which would lead to the crown prince discussion. I can't expect a woman like Sam to want to give up her life to be with me. Why did I think even think about that? I barely know her, so it's much too soon to worry about whether she wants to become my princess.

Sam leads me into the shop and takes my hand to guide me over to the selection of snowsuits hanging on a rack. Thankfully, I see most of them are available in masculine colors as well as pink and lavender. I don't think lavender is my color. So I try on a tan suit.

"What do you think?" I ask Sam as I turn in a circle. "Am I fashionable?"

She gives me the okay sign with her fingers. "You're the best dressed Brit in New England. But you're missing one thing." She hurries over to a shelf of knit hats and returns to pull one onto my head. She smiles brightly. "Perfect."

The hat is tan, like my snowsuit, but it also features a puffy yellow ball on top and two knit straps that hang down and have puffy yellow balls on their ends. The girl is teasing me again, and I love it.

She pulls out her mobile, aiming it at me. "Mind if I take a picture?"

"Go on. You can't embarrass me this way. I've been forced to wear much sillier outfits."

"Really?" She snaps a picture, then stashes her mobile in the pocket of her coat. "What kind of silly outfits?"

"Maybe I'll tell you later, after I've gotten some dirt on you too."

"Fair enough." She bites her lip. "Hate to leave you all alone in a strange place, but I desperately need to use the restroom."

"Go on. I'm not helpless on my own."

While Sam trots off to wherever the loo is, I do a quick visual survey of the store. If they have condoms here, where would I find them? I spot a display in the far corner that looks promising, so I hurry over there, in a way that hopefully doesn't look like I'm a sex-starved moron who's rushing over to the condom display. But I do find them there, amongst the toothbrushes and wet wipes.

Now, if I can only work up the nerve to seduce that girl again…

Chapter Six

Ben is up to something. I can tell by the way he keeps glancing at me sideways and staring at my breasts when he thinks I'm not looking. Does he want to have sex again? I'd love to do that, and go all the way this time, but I didn't think about buying condoms back in the Discount Depot. I shouldn't want to get naked with him since we just met and I don't do casual hookups.

Until last night. Something about Ben turns me into a sex-crazed lunatic. In my experience, sweet and sexy is the hottest combination. Every time Ben smiles at me, I want to melt into a puddle at his feet. But when he leans in to whisper in my ear, I swear I go weak in the knees. It's crazy. Nobody actually gets weak in the knees from desire.

But I do. With him.

The things he whispers aren't dirty either. He tells me how much he wants to try New England cuisine and that he'd love to return the favor and show me his home in England. Of course, every time he says the name Cockshire, I want to laugh and then mount him like a wild thing.

We eat lunch at the Crab Cottage, which has good food that's not super fancy. Ben lights up when he sees the decor—semi-cheesy nautical knickknacks. We wind up sitting at a table situated right under a large fish mounted on a wood plaque. I have no idea what kind of fish that is, so when Ben asks me about that, I can't resist having a little fun with him.

"It's an abyssal carp," I say in my best deadpan. "Better not get too close. They're carnivorous and have been known to revive from death, even after being stuffed and mounted, to latch on to an unsuspecting tourist's throat."

Ben folds his arms over his chest and leans back, eying me with a slight smirk. "Hmm, I think you're having me on."

"You're confused. I had you last night."

"True. But having me on means you're teasing me again."

"It's completely your fault that I keep teasing you."

His smirk slides into a playful smile. "How is it my fault?"

"Because you're so damn cute and sexy. I have to poke fun at you because if I don't, we'll wind up naked on the floor in this restaurant."

"Is public nudity not illegal in America?"

"Probably is. But I'm sure public sex is."

His gaze falls to my chest, and his tongue slides across his bottom lip. "I bought condoms."

I freeze. Yeah, that statement came completely out of the blue. Well, maybe not completely. I did just suggest I want to screw him on the floor right next to our table. Ben Montague turns me into a lunatic.

He bought condoms. That means… Oh, I am in so much trouble.

Suddenly, I feel warm and tingly in ways that are not appropriate in public.

"I know I shouldn't," Ben says, his voice deeper and huskier, "but I want you, Sam. Want you like mad."

My mouth opens, but before I can speak, the waitress arrives with our food. Saved by crab cakes and cod fillets. Well, I'm saved until the waitress leaves and he speaks again.

Ben leans forward and murmurs in that husky tone, "I need to shag you right now, Samantha."

My pulse revs into overdrive, and I'm so wet and tingly between my thighs that I have trouble catching my breath. Maybe if he hadn't spoken my full name, I could resist this insane and inappropriate lust. But he did say it. And I need to shag *him* right now too.

"We can't have sex in a restaurant," I say, though my breathless tone doesn't sound at all convincing.

"No one can see us here, in this secluded corner."

And we're sitting in a semicircular booth. I could slide across the vinyl, climb onto his lap, and…

I've lost my mind, for sure. But I don't care anymore. What has being a good girl gotten me? Cheated on, taken for granted, dumped again and again. Men can be such dicks. But this man is fun and sweet, and he'll be leaving as soon as the roads are clear. That means I can do something wild with him and no one will ever know. I won't see him again. Whatever we do together will stay a secret between us.

Or maybe I'm rationalizing my desperate need to screw Ben's brains out.

I grab my fork and stare down at my plate. "Mm, this looks yummy."

Though I say that as if I'm starved for the food on my plate, it's really him I need to devour. I've never thought of seafood as erotic, but right now, I can't think of anything other than sex. I could smear tartar sauce all over Ben's naked body and—*No, cut that out, woman. You will not "shag" Ben in this booth.*

God, I want to do that.

Ben spears a forkful of cod and slides it between his lips. He chews with leisure, his gaze pinned to mine, his jaw working. I flash back to last night when he had his head between my legs and his mouth on me. His jaw had worked in the same way as it does now, though he'd been consuming me instead of a slab of fish.

I should've taken him to a German restaurant and ordered sauerkraut for both of us. No way I could get turned on by that. Right? *Ugh.* I doubt it matters what he eats. I'll want him even with garlic breath and jalapeno juice on his lips.

Ben lifts his water glass and takes a big gulp. Then he licks his lips and groans. "Delicious."

What happened to sweet Ben who was embarrassed for me to see him naked? Now, he's seducing me in a seafood restaurant. And the way he groaned a minute ago made me so wet my panties are damp. My sex throbbed too.

A girl only has so much willpower.

I slide across the curved booth until I'm sitting right next to Ben. Then I slant toward him so my lips brush his ear, and I whisper, "You said you bought condoms. But did you bring one with you?"

"Yes." He pulls a foil packet out of his pocket. "I wouldn't have mentioned condoms if I didn't have one on me."

"Good. I'm so hot for you I can't wait till we get back to my place."

"I can't wait either."

He slides his free hand into my hair, tugging my face closer to his, and seals his mouth over mine. I can't help moaning. His lips feel so good, and when he pushes his tongue into my mouth, I sag against him. He teases and tastes me, wrapping his tongue around mine only to withdraw it, while his breaths tickle my skin and arouse every fine hair. I thrust my tongue between his lips to devour him with wild lashes, and the tingling between my thighs rushes over my entire body.

Ben pulls away, though only a little. "You're wearing trousers."

"I know."

"That, ah, might pose a problem if we're going to shag right now."

"Problem-solving is my forte." I kick off my boots, then unzip my pants and shimmy out of them and my panties while still sitting on the bench. Setting them down beside me, I spread my thighs. "See? No problem."

Can't believe I just stripped in a restaurant. Sure, my upper body is covered, but I'm naked from the waist down. Well, except for my socks.

Ben unzips his pants and eases his dick free of them. I watch while he rips open the condom packet and rolls the latex over his length.

"How long have you been hard?" I ask.

"I started to get randy as soon as we sat down here." He lays a hand on my thigh, sliding it up until his fingers graze my mound. "I know it's insane, but I can't stop wanting you."

"Same for me. I'm obsessed with the idea of feeling you inside me."

He pushes his fingers between my folds, petting my slick flesh. "Need to fuck you now, Sam."

Oh God, I need that too. So I swing my leg over his lap and kneel astride him, then lower my body onto his cock. The feel of him gliding into me, filling me up, makes me suck in a breath and grip his shoulders. He grasps my hips, urging me to move, and I can't resist anything he wants. I rock my hips, rise up only to slam back down, and dig my fingers into his shoulders while I get more and more excited, breathing so hard I'm panting. He groans and latches on to my nipple through my sweater and bra, but despite the barrier, my stiff peak feels damp from his mouth and lightning bolts of pleasure fire down my nerves from my nipple straight into my core.

I wrap my arms around his neck, my lips grazing his ear. "Oh Ben, yes, you feel so damn good."

"Samantha, you're so hot and wet, I can't—Ah, fuck."

He thrusts his hips up as I drop down, driving his cock even deeper inside me. I feel the orgasm building, tightening everything inside me, shortening my breaths, quickening my pulse. I hug him tightly with my face mashed to his neck to muffle the cry I know will explode out of me when I come.

Ben shoves a hand between our bodies to rub my clit.

I sink my teeth into his neck while my body convulses around him, milking his cock until he comes deep inside me, stifling his own cry while I whimper and struggle not to scream. Not making too much noise intensifies everything, and I come even harder.

Once the climax fades, I slump against Ben. I can't manage more than a whisper when I say, "Wow, that was amazing."

He rubs his hands over my back. "Definitely incredible."

I lift my head, intending to look into Ben's eyes, but something else catches my attention.

The waitress has just walked out of the hallway that leads to this secluded part of the restaurant. She stands frozen in the entryway, eyes bulging, mouth open—and she stares straight at me and Ben.

Oh shit.

Chapter Seven

Ben

I can't believe that just happened. Can't believe I suggested we have sex in this restaurant, where anyone might see us—and I absolutely cannot believe Sam said yes. We're both off our trolleys, aren't we? Ever since I first saw my savior in pink, I've behaved like a lunatic. It must be stress. I ran away from my life so fast, without making any concrete plans, that I'm feeling a bit off-balance. That's the only excuse I have for the fact I seduced this woman twice in less than twenty-four hours.

Sam is still straddling my lap, and I'm still inside her. But something past my shoulder seems to have caught her attention. Her eyes go wide, and her lips fall open.

Is that shock on her face? Twisting my head around, I try to see what stunned her.

Our waitress hovers on the threshold between the hallway and this little hidden corner. The girl gapes at us with even more shock than Sam shows on her face. Bloody hell. That waitress must have seen us going at it. This booth is set away from the rest of the restaurant, but anyone could've peeked through the doorways at either end and seen us. Anyone who wants to use the loo has to walk past our booth.

The waitress hurries away, out of sight.

Sam slides off my lap and struggles to reassemble her clothes. "What should we do? Leave? Or pretend that didn't happen?"

"Don't know about you, but I can't pretend we didn't do that." I stuff the used condom in my pocket and zip up my trousers. "Why don't you, ah, go back around to your side of the table."

"Oh. Sure. Good idea." She scrambles to get back to the spot where her food waits for her. Then she picks up her fork and freezes, as if she's forgotten what to do with it.

"Are you all right?" I ask. Should I not have ordered her to go back over there? Maybe I was meant to hold her and whisper to her about how wonderful she is. Bollocks. I should've done that, right? I'm an idiot, and now she feels uncomfortable. "Sorry, I—You could come back over here if you like."

She bites her upper lip and shifts her gaze to me while keeping her head down. "I'm okay here."

But I'm not entirely convinced she is. What we just did has scrambled my brain, though, and I can't think of a bloody thing to say that won't sound stupid. So I opt for what might be the worst possible response, but it's all I can think of.

I start eating again. Shoveling it in, actually.

Sam stares at me, seeming not to blink.

"Aren't you hungry?" I say with my mouth full. I'm bloody starving.

"Uh, yeah, sure." She slides a tiny bit of food onto her fork and daintily sets it on her tongue. While she chews, she keeps watching me cram cod and crab cakes into my mouth. "What's wrong with you?"

"Nothing. I'm fine. Why?" *You sodding liar.*

"You'll get indigestion if you keep eating that fast."

"I've got an iron constitution." No idea if that's true, since never in my life have I eaten this much this fast. I swallow another half-chewed mouthful. "Are you all right? I didn't mean to shove you away. Just thought we should, uh, separate before someone else saw us."

"Separate?" she says with a snort. "Guess that's the British way of saying it."

"Of saying what?"

"That you wish we hadn't done that."

I drop my fork, and it clatters onto my plate. "How can you think I regret it?"

Sam hunches her shoulders. "You did push me away."

"No, I—" Yes, of course that's what I did. Why am I lying about it? "Sorry. I shouldn't have treated you that way. But I've never had sex in a public place before. I guess I'm feeling…odd about the whole thing. It was brilliant, but—"

"You can stop talking now, Ben. I get what you mean. I've never done anything like that either." Her gaze flicks to something past my shoulder. When I look, no one is there. Sam sighs and shakes her head, focusing on me again. "Can't believe I did that, but I don't regret having sex with you. I regret that the waitress saw us."

"Me too. Sorry we got caught, but not sorry we did that."

"Glad we straightened that out. Now, let's eat and talk about anything except sex."

"Absolutely."

We do just that—finish our meal and chat to each other about inconsequential things like whether crab cakes are better than cod, or how many pieces of garlic bread we can eat in one minute. Sam claims she can eat four pieces. When I make a sarcastically dismissive noise, she announces she will prove it to me. But I tell her not to bother. I take her word for it, no proof necessary.

How many girls would want to eat that much garlic bread? Sam has a healthy appetite and doesn't seem to care what anyone thinks of her. I love that about her. When I'm in Cockshire with my mates, I feel free. But when I go home to Mithoria, I remember all the reasons I can't be free, not when everyone has expectations that have nothing whatever to do with me. No one cares what I want. I have a duty, full stop. But when I'm with Sam, none of that matters. I feel even freer with her than with my mates, and I don't want to lose whatever this is that seems to be growing between us. I know I met her last night, but I already feel more myself than I ever have. Maybe that's why I keep seducing her. If I shag her twenty-four hours a day, maybe I'll never need to go home.

As we're leaving the restaurant, our waitress waves to Sam as if she wants to talk to her. I wait while the two women speak to each other in hushed voices that I can't understand. Then Sam comes back to me.

"She wanted to let us know," Sam says in that same hushed tone, "that she won't tell anybody what she saw and she doesn't think anyone else saw it."

"Oh. Good."

"Would you like to see anything else in town? Or should we just go back to my place?"

If we do that, I'll fuck her again. Can't control myself when I'm with her. That probably means I need intensive therapy, but I don't care. Still, I should avoid being alone with her for a while, until my libido has recovered from restaurant sex. We should've at least done it in a posh restaurant with wine, soft lighting, and piano music in the background.

"What else is there to do in lovely North Slipperton?" I ask.

"There's an outdoor skating rink."

"I don't know how to skate."

She hooks her arm around mine, her cheeks dimpling with a sweet smile. "I'll teach you."

"All right. But maybe we should go back to the Discount Depot so I can buy knee pads and elbow pads, probably head protection too."

"You'll be fine. Trust me."

Strangely, I do trust her.

And so I let Samantha Lockhart drag me to the skating rink. Mostly, I see parents watching from the perimeter while their children glide across the ice, some of them even doing acrobatic moves like leaping up and twirling. Not sure what the official terms are for those moves. I've never been interested in sports of any kind, so I couldn't even explain rugby to Sam if she asked me about it. Most of my mates love football, though I know Americans call it soccer. That's the extent of my knowledge about the sport. Dane Dixon loves bowls, but I know even less about that game. I think it involves rolling one ball into another very slowly.

I hope Sam doesn't ask me about sports. Telling her I'm awful at that rubbish because I have zero interest in it might convince her I'm a useless twat. Or do women prefer men who aren't into sports? I have no idea.

Sam rents us skates, but she has to help me put mine on. I can't figure out how to lace them up.

"At least you didn't get me pink skates," I say while watching her tie my laces.

"You have a phobia about that color, don't you?"

"No, not a phobia. Pink is for girls."

"Oh, I see." She glances up to smirk at me. "You're not uptight, you're a sexist."

I hope she doesn't really think I'm uptight. After our restaurant encounter, I don't see how she could think that. She must be teasing me again.

Sam pats my ankle. "You're all set."

Now if I can just stay on my feet and not fall on my arse in front of the most beautiful woman I've ever met...

I follow Sam onto the ice, though I cling to the wooden barrier that surrounds the rink. She takes hold of my arm, encouraging me to push away from the wall. This isn't too difficult. I might be wobbling a bit, but I manage to keep myself upright. Sam gives me pointers and offers encouragement. How many women would take the time to teach me how to skate? A little girl half my size bumps into me while she's executing some kind of spinning jump. I don't fall over, and the girl shyly apologizes. A child that size can leap around like an Olympic athlete? I have trouble staying on my feet—or rather, my blades—without my legs flipping out from under me.

"You're doing great," Sam says while smiling at me. "You're picking it up in no time."

"There's no need to patronize me. My ego isn't that fragile."

"Not patronizing you. I mean every word."

And I believe she does. Sam is wonderful.

She grins and waggles her eyebrows. "Wanna try a triple axel?"

"Depends. What is a triple axel?"

"A jump. You leap up and spin around three times fast while holding a specific position. I'm no expert, but I watch a lot of figure skating on TV."

"I see. Well, we should only do that if you want to pick up the pieces of my shattered bones afterward."

"You are such a pessimist."

"Are you going to do one of those axel whatsits?"

"Oh no, not me. I'd break my neck for sure."

I bump my shoulder into her. "Now who's a pessimist?"

"How about hot cocoa instead of a triple axel?"

"Now that's a sport I can handle."

She laughs. "Drinking cocoa is a sport?"

"Of course it is. The perfect sip is an art form."

I'm completely full of rubbish, but she doesn't care. That's one of the things I love most about her. Sam enjoys being silly and listening to me spout bollocks just to make her smile.

"Let's go back to your house," I say. "Had enough of exploring the town for one day."

"Sure thing. Just let me grab a few things from the grocery store."

We return our skates and walk down the main street—which might actually be called Main Street, but I'm not sure. Hand in hand, we stroll past the businesses that line the pavement and admire the window displays of various shops. This town is bigger than I expected, though it's no metropolis. I like that. Cockshire isn't a large place either, and I feel comfortable there.

"How do you like North Slipperton so far?" Sam asks as we amble past a sweets shop.

"It's lovely."

"Not too teeny for you?"

"Are you under the impression I live in a big city? I don't. Cockshire is a small village."

She stops us at a window display of handmade leather purses, but she looks at me instead of the items in the window. "Have you ever lived in a city?"

"I went to university in a city, but by the time I graduated, I'd had enough of that lifestyle. When I got a job working as a massage therapist in Cockshire, I realized country life is what I want."

"Me too. I used to live in Philadelphia, but I got sick of the city."

Another thing we have in common. The more I learn about her, the more I want to know. So I ask a bloody stupid question. "How do you find men to date when you live in the middle of nowhere?"

"I haven't dated anyone since I moved here. Told you last night I'm taking a break from that stuff."

Right. She did tell me that. Since it was during our attempt to have sex, I sort of forgot.

"Why are you taking a break from dating?" I ask. "I imagine the dating pool is rather small in North Slipperton, but there is online dating."

"Have you ever tried that? It's awful." She finally aims her gaze at the window display, though I don't think she's actually looking at it. "Besides, I had enough of men for a good long while."

"Bad breakup?"

"Not just one. Several." She sighs, and her expression turns melancholy. "Maybe there's something wrong with me, I don't know. But men always disappoint me."

"There's nothing wrong with you." I release her hand so I can wrap my arm around her shoulders. "You are a wonderful girl."

"You're very sweet, Ben. But you don't really know me."

And she doesn't really know me either. Should I tell her about my family? No, it's much too soon to drop that bomb on her head. I can't imagine she would lustfully hunger for the status and wealth my family can offer, but I don't want to scare her away. Am I sort of, potentially, considering that she might become my girlfriend? No, I can't do that. She loves her simple life here in New Hampshire, and I would never want to drag her away from that.

My world is no place for a kind, sweet woman like Sam.

Why did I run away from that world? While I follow Sam back to where we left her snowmobile, I can't help wondering if she could handle knowing who and what I am. But if I tell her, and she runs away like a ravenous bear is chasing her…

No, I shouldn't tell her anything. I don't want her to get entangled in my world. It would only wreck her life.

<h1 style="text-align:center">Chapter Eight</h1>

Sam

Ben gets quiet once we're back at my place and seems kind of depressed. He started seeming that way before we left town, but I couldn't ask him about it since a snowmobile ride isn't conducive to talking. Once we get inside my house, he says he needs to lie down for a while because he's "knackered," which I assume means he's wiped out. Ben retreats to the sofa and stretches out lengthwise, grabbing the fleece blanket I keep on the sofa's back and draping it over his eyes and nose with only his mouth visible. Then he clasps his hands over his belly.

And he pretends to sleep.

Yeah, I'm pretty sure he's playing possum. His breathing doesn't slow down the way it does when someone falls asleep, and he occasionally twiddles his thumbs.

Why did Ben need to lie down and hide under a blanket? I decide my best option is to wait until he gives up the farce and wants to talk to me again. Maybe he's embarrassed by what we did in the restaurant. I should probably feel that way, but I don't. If any other man had suggested getting it on in public, I would've told him N-O in a big way. But I can't say no to Ben. I suppose I should worry about why that is, but I can't do that either. He is hands-down the sexiest sweetie-pie I've ever met.

While Ben pretends to sleep, I go out on the deck to check on the hot tub. Grandpa had loved to soak in there during the cold winter months, and he placed the hot tub on the side of the house that rarely gets much wind. That means the blizzard yesterday probably didn't cover the hot tub with three feet of snow. But I should make sure everything's okay out there.

All I need to do is spend a few minutes shoveling away the little bit of snow that accumulated around the hot tub. Its cover protected it from the elements, so I'll be good to go if I want to enjoy a soak in the outdoors.

Does Ben like hot tubs? I'd love to relax in the steamy water with him.

With that thought in mind, I remove the cover and turn on the jets. I've got an intuition that we'll be using this tub later—because I'm going to suggest it.

When I walk into the living room again, Ben has given up feigning sleep. He's sitting up and stretching his arms above his head while a slight smile curves his lips.

"Feeling better?" I ask as I sit on the sofa beside him. "You seemed a little bummed earlier."

He lifts his brows. "Bummed? No, I wouldn't characterize it as that. I was tired."

"But you faked being asleep."

He winces a teeny bit. "Sorry. I didn't want to talk, but I was actually tired. Just not ready to sleep."

"It's okay. We aren't dating, so you're under no obligation to share your deepest feelings with me."

"But I want to share things with you." He angles toward me, laying his arm across the sofa's back. "I like you a lot, Sam. But my, ah, family situation is rather complicated."

"Don't you get along with your family?"

"We get on all right. But I have…obligations that have become sort of an albatross around my neck." He sighs. "I love my mum and dad, and my sister, but everyone expects me to give up the life I've built for myself just so I can fulfill some arbitrary duty."

Oh yeah, my curiosity just kicked into high gear. But I shouldn't ask intrusive questions. It's not my business. So I say the only thing that seems acceptable under the circumstances. "I'm sorry you're stressed, Ben. Wish I could make you feel better."

"You have. Meeting you has been a breath of fresh air."

"That's so sweet of you to say. And I feel the same way about you." I turn toward him, tucking my feet under me cross-legged. "Like I mentioned earlier, men have disappointed me so many times that I've been taking an extended vacation from dating. That's why I moved out here. I needed a break from all the craziness of city life and the social scene. My old job became so stressful that I needed to get away, at least for a while."

"You're not permanently living here."

"Not sure yet. I do love the area, but sometimes I get lonely."

"I know the feeling." He veers his gaze away from me. "You can be surrounded by people and still be lonely, though. I have mates who are amazing, but I've never found… I don't know. Sometimes I feel like there's something missing in my life, but I don't know what it is."

"You said you're stressed because of your family obligations. Maybe what you've been missing is time to kick back and forget about all that."

He looks at me and smiles. "Are you inviting me to kick back with you?"

"Isn't that what we've been doing? I mean, that and screwing each other." I lean in to give him a quick kiss. "But I guess sex is part of relaxation. Right?"

"Certainly makes me feel more relaxed."

I scoot closer to him. "Wanna play a game?"

"What did you have in mind?"

"Go fish." I slant forward to whisper in his ear, "Strip go fish."

"Strip? Never heard of doing that with go fish, but I'm up for anything with you."

"Ben, you are so unbelievably sweet and hot."

"So are you."

I hop off the sofa. "While I find a deck of cards, you can get us something to drink."

He heads for the kitchen while I go to my room to rummage around in the big closet. I know I've got cards in here somewhere, but since I haven't had any reason to get them out in a long time, it takes me a while to hunt them down. Finally, I dig them out and return to the living room, where Ben sits on the sofa again.

Two bottles of root beer sit on the coffee table.

"Root beer?" I say as I settle onto the sofa beside him. "I assumed you'd pick something sexy like wine."

"I want you sober while I beat you at strip go fish." He smirks. "Because I plan to fuck you afterward. Or possibly during the game. Maybe both."

"Boy, I had no idea I picked up a sex fiend on the road last night. You seemed like such a nice, clean-cut guy."

"Every man is a fiend at heart. We can't help it. Women drive us barmy."

I pretend to be offended, clucking my tongue. "So you're blaming women? I may have to lock you in the basement until you change your ways."

"Lock me up anywhere you like, love."

A delicious shiver tingles over my skin when he calls me "love." No man has ever called me that before. I've been referred to as "hon" and "sweetie," but that was by elderly gentlemen, not guys I dated. I suppose "love" is a British thing, more like saying hello than an endearment, so I shouldn't get too excited about it.

But everything about Ben gets me excited.

His gaze wanders to the mantel over the fireplace. "Why do you have seven stockings?"

"For me, my parents, my brother and his wife, and their two daughters. I put the stockings up as a way to… I don't know. Feel closer to them, I guess, even though they aren't here."

"Why aren't you visiting them for Christmas?"

"Thought I wanted to be alone. Until you turned up."

"Yeah, I thought the same thing. Until you rescued me."

I bring out the cards and shuffle them. "Sure you can handle getting your butt whupped by a girl? I'm awesome at go fish."

"My sister and I used to play this game when we were little. Stephanie hated to lose, which meant she was always annoyed after our tournaments."

"You played go fish tournaments?"

"Of course. It wasn't a hobby. It was war." He rests an arm on the sofa's back. "But my mother was the reigning champion. Sometimes after I beat Steph, Dad would play me and kick my arse. Then Mum would insist on showing Dad how the game should be played. No one beats Mum at go fish."

I can't help laughing. "I have got to meet your family sometime. They sound like a hoot."

The excitement floods out of his expression, and the light in his eyes dims. His shoulders droop. "Forgot how much fun we used to have. It's been a long time since we've done anything like that."

"That's too bad. Sounds like it was amazing. But maybe you guys can play go fish again when you get home."

He bows his head, and his voice gets softer. "My family doesn't live in England. They're…further away."

"Oh. When did you last see them?"

"Last week."

If he saw his family last week, why does he seem so sad when she talks about them? I know it's none of my business, which means I should lock my curiosity up in a little box in my head. If he wants to tell me, he will.

So instead of grilling him, I deal the cards. "You can go first."

He examines the cards I gave him. "Do you have any queens?"

"Nope. Go fish."

Ben doesn't get a queen that way either, which means he loses that hand. "I suppose it's time for me to remove an article of clothing."

"You can start with your socks if you want."

"No, I like to start big." He whips his shirt off and flings it aside. "Socks go last."

Maybe a part of me expected him to feel uncomfortable with stripping in front of me. He did get embarrassed last night when I accidentally caught him in the nude. But earlier, we did something very inappropriate in a restaurant, at his suggestion, so I shouldn't have assumed anything about him. Ben isn't shy. He might be soft-spoken at times and very polite in general, but he has a naughty streak too.

I love that about him.

"Your turn," Ben says. Then he glances at my breasts. "You'll be taking your shirt off in a few seconds."

"Don't get cocky. You just lost the first hand."

"Maybe I did that on purpose so I could get you randy by showing off my chest."

"You do have a great set of pecs and abs." I focus on my cards, chewing my lip while I mull my options. "Do you have any fours?"

"Bloody hell," he groans as he hands me two fours. "How did you know? Do you have a mirror hidden somewhere behind me?"

"No," I say with a laugh. "Just a good guess. You don't handle losing very well, do you?"

"Haven't lost yet. Not until I have no cards left."

"Or no clothes left."

"Good point."

Since it's still my turn, I ask him, "Got any jacks?"

"Ha! No, I don't have a single ruddy jack." He waves his hand in a sweeping gesture aimed at my chest. "Off with your shirt, please."

"Maybe I'll start with my socks."

"Oh no. I took off my shirt, so you have to do the same."

"I don't think that's in the rules."

He rolls his eyes. "Stripping isn't in the rules, full stop. Now take off your shirt, Sam. Please."

"Well, since you said please…" I slowly unbutton my shirt while his gaze tracks the movements of my fingers. He licks his lips when I've unhooked the last button. I peel my shirt off and toss it onto the coffee table. "Satisfied?"

"Not yet. But I will be later." He lifts his gaze to mine. "When I'm fucking you again after I've won this tournament."

"Competitive, aren't you?"

"Not usually." He puckers his lips while he studies his cards. "Give me all your sevens."

Damn. I have a seven. That means I won't get to see more of Ben until it's my turn again. I hand the card over, and he smiles with smug satisfaction. He only won the hand, not the game. But he's so darn cute when he's trying to beat the socks off me, literally. I start losing hands on purpose just for an excuse to remove more of my clothing, and I suspect Ben might be doing the same thing since he asks if I have sixes when he must realize he's already given me as many as there are in the deck. He must know I've done the same thing.

Yeah, we're having way too much fun making each other strip. Who cares? This is a vacation for both of us, and we deserve to have a good time.

But my thoughts keep circling back around to the hot tub.

Chapter Nine

Ben

By the time we're out of cards, Sam has won the game. I'm naked, but she still has her knickers on, which seems unfair. Sure, she's about ninety-seven percent naked, but I wanted to get her to one hundred percent. Of course, I've seen her nude body before. But I guess it's my hidden competitive streak rearing its head and demanding I do something to remedy the situation and get her to take off those skimpy little knickers.

They're pink lace, naturally.

"Are you obsessed with pink?" I ask. "I would've expected you to have pink walls in here, and pink kitchen utensils."

"Ha-ha. I'm not obsessed. I like pink, that's all. For clothing only, though. Well, that and my snowmobile."

"I see." My gaze returns to her groin and those blasted knickers that hide the part of her I want to fondle and kiss. "We need to have another tournament, so I can get you to take off your underwear."

"You'd lose, buddy. I'd wipe the floor with you again."

She probably would. I don't care as long as I can get her completely naked. Desperation turns me into a liar. "In England, it's the custom for the loser in a game of cards to get one request. The winner can't deny it, no matter what the request is."

The girl I need to shag again laughs at me. "You are so full of it, Ben. I don't believe for one second that Brits have a rule like that."

"Maybe it's only the Brits who live in Cockshire that have a rule about card games."

"Uh-huh. Still not buying it."

Her gaze drops to my groin—to my cock, actually. It is rousing, thanks to her. Yes, it's Sam's fault I'm getting an erection. She shouldn't be mostly naked while teasing me. I can't help the fact that her attention on that part of me makes my body respond.

Yes, all right, I'm having the best time of my life here in a cabin in the woods in New Hampshire. The woman mocking me is the reason for that. I don't want to go home, not only because "home" means going back to Mithoria, but also because I love being here with Sam.

She rises onto her knees and waddles toward me until her pink lace knickers hover inches from my face. "There's a simple solution to the problem."

"You're referring to the issue of your knickers."

"Mm-hm." She rocks her hips forward, pushing her groin closer to my face. "Tear them off, Ben."

"Tearing fabric isn't as easy as they make it look in movies. Believe me, I've tried it."

"You've tried to rip a woman's underwear off?"

"No. It was a pair of socks that shrunk in the laundry, and I tried to tear them into pieces to make dishrags out of them. All I accomplished was cutting myself with my own fingernail."

Why did I tell her that? It's an embarrassing story, not the sort that would make her mad with lust for me.

She ruffles my hair, laughing softly. "You're adorable. Do you know that? Trust me, these 'knickers' are flimsy, and you can rip them off no problem."

"If I cut myself with my fingernail again, my injury will be your fault."

"Don't worry. I've got a first aid kit." She kisses the top of my head. "I'll be your nurse and make sure you feel all better."

I take hold of her knickers with both hands and yank. The fabric rips. With two more yanks, I've gotten rid of the pink lace, which now lies on the coffee table alongside other items of our clothing. "Thank goodness. Now I feel like a man again. In fact, I'm fairly sure I can brag about this to my mates for at least a month."

"They suck at tearing women's clothes off?"

"No idea. I've never discussed that with them."

She slides her hands into my hair. "You rock the clothes ripping. That was so macho and sexy."

"I can honestly say no one has ever called me macho before."

"Have you ever made love in the water?" She sits down, straddling my lap. "Because I've got a hot tub."

"Never been in one of those before."

"Should we try it?"

"Yes, please, right now." I might've sounded a little too excited about the hot tub, but I don't care. The thought of fucking her in the water makes me so randy that I can't think straight. Can't think in squiggly lines either.

"Let's do it," Sam says. Then she climbs off my lap to stand beside me with her hand outstretched. "Come on, Ben. Let's get dirty in the hot tub."

We race out of the house hand in hand, heading onto the covered porch that houses the hot tub. It's bloody cold out here, but I don't care about the temperature anymore once we both jump into the steaming water. We splash that water all over the porch, but Sam tells me not to worry about creating ice since she'll just "sprinkle some ice melt on there later." I have to ask what ice melt is, but she doesn't think I'm stupid for not knowing. Her explanation doesn't clear up the whole issue, since she calls it "crystallized stuff that makes ice go away."

I decide the full explanation doesn't matter. After all, I've got naked Sam in the hot tub with me while jets make bubbles all around us. Her tits bob in the current from the jets.

Yes, I could get used to living like this.

I slip an arm around Sam's waist and pull her closer. "You look even sexier when you're wet."

"Not completely wet, though." She grins and ducks her head under the water, then bobs back up. "Now I am. Want to see my underwater trick?"

"Love to. Are you going to perform a synchronized swimming routine in this little pool?"

"You'll see."

She plunges under the water again, but through the bubbles, I can't tell exactly what she's trying to do down there. The jets make her hair rise like a golden curtain in front of me. Her fingers curl around my cock, gliding up and down, and I sag against the tub while my eyes drift half-closed. Oh yes, I could do more than get used to this life. I may never want to leave.

I groan when she closes her mouth around me.

Why would I want to marry an obnoxious aristocratic girl when I could stay here with a woman who's sweet and sexy and loves to give me head in a hot tub? I'd have to be insane to give this up.

Sam works my cock with her mouth and hands while I hiss and groan, sliding a hand into her hair to cup the back of her head. Fuck, she's amazing. I may not feel quite as relaxed now, but the tension building inside me feels wonderful. She pops her head out of the water to smile at me while she takes a few slow breaths.

Then she dives back in, and her lips and tongue surround me again.

I lean forward, sliding a hand down her back until I can push my fingers between her arse cheeks and down into her cleft, where I find the stiff head of her clitoris. Pushing my thumb inside her, I rub that little button.

She pops up out of the water, breathing hard.

I'm still rubbing her.

"That was so hot," she says as she wriggles away from my hand. "But I'll drown trying to go all the way and make you come in my mouth." She tickles my chest. "Especially with you touching me like that."

"Couldn't help myself."

She glances around like she's searching for something. "Don't suppose you have a condom on you."

"I ran out here in the nude. So no, I didn't think to grab one." I start to turn around, intending to haul myself out of the water. "I'll do that now."

She lays a hand on my chest and pushes me back down. "Let me get the condom. Where are you keeping them?"

"In my suitcase. The big one."

"You stay right here and think filthy thoughts about me." She plants her palms on the tub's edge and hoists her body out of the water. Then she leans in to whisper to me, "You better still be hard when I get back."

"That's a certainty."

As soon as she disappears into the house, I realize she might have trouble finding that box of condoms. I'd stuffed them into my suitcase under my clothes. Not sure why I did that, but it had seemed like a good idea at the time. I climb out of the tub and grab one of the towels lying on a wooden chair, neatly folded, as if they're waiting for us. Sam must've put those towels there earlier. I quickly dry myself off and sling the towel around my waist, then trot into the house.

I bump into Sam on the threshold between the hallway and the living room. I literally bump into her. She veers into the hall just as I reach the threshold and runs into me. Yelping, she stumbles backward a step.

"You scared me," she says, laying a hand on her chest. "Thought you were waiting for me in the hot tub."

"I suddenly realized you might have trouble finding the condoms."

"Nope." She lifts the box. "No trouble at all. I had to dig around in your underwear, but I didn't figure you'd mind."

"You can rummage in my underwear anytime you like."

She's still naked, but I don't mind that either.

I hear a mobile ringing and realize it's mine. "Sorry. I should check that in case it's important."

Maybe I shouldn't check. After all, it could be my mother. Well, she has no idea where I am, so it's not like she can hunt me down if I answer the call. Besides, the screen will tell me who's ringing me.

"Go on," Sam says. "Answer your phone. It's cool."

"I'll be quick, promise."

Walking away from a wet, naked woman who wants to shag me doesn't seem like the cleverest idea. But I act like a good boy and rush over to the bar where I'd left my mobile. And I answer it.

"Sorry to bother you," Chance Dixon says, "but Elena wanted to make sure you remembered to water the plants."

Oh bollocks. He thinks I'm at his house in Hartmoor.

"Ah, there's been a change of plans," I say. "I took a wrong turn and got lost, then I sort of got stuck in a blizzard. The roads are still closed, so I can't get to your house yet. I hope the plants will survive."

"Where are you staying?"

"I made a new friend, and I'm staying at her cabin near North Slipperton."

"Ah, I see. Well, at least you're not lonely."

The tone of his voice suggests what he means is "have fun shagging that girl you just met and don't forget the condom." Chance would never say that to me so baldly. He's a lawyer, so he prefers to couch his statements in vague terms. Besides, everyone loves to harass me about the fact that I don't have a girlfriend at the moment.

Does Sam count? We're getting a leg over as often as possible, but I'm not sure that counts as dating. Of course, we did have lunch together, so...

"Are you still there, mate?" Chance asks.

"Yes. Sorry. Did you just call to check on the plants?"

"No. I also thought you should know that your mother is convinced Nick and Siobhan are hiding you. In his closet or maybe in the garage. Not sure which. She might interrogate Nick in person, or she might call in a favor somewhere and have Interpol hunt you down."

"Interpol? I'm not an international crime lord."

"No, you're something much worse." He lowers his voice to a sarcastic whisper. "An escaped crown prince with a mother who will scour the earth to find you."

"Bloody hell. I only left Mithoria a week ago. And I left a note."

"Apparently, whatever you wrote did not appease her."

"Tell Nick I'm sorry. I'll sort this, I swear."

"Don't worry. Nick can handle himself." Chance pauses, then asks, "What about this new friend of yours? Is she a potential princess?"

"I met her yesterday." And I've already had sex with her two and a half times. Or maybe it's one and three quarters, considering that we didn't go all the way the first time. "I'll tell you more about that later. Cheers, Chance."

"Cheers, Ben."

I set my mobile down on the bar and turn around.

Sam is standing near the sofa, still naked. "Should we finish what we started in the hot tub?"

"Yes, absolutely."

We both grin.

The doorbell rings.

Sam groans, her shoulders sagging. "That might be important. I'd better grab a robe."

I watch her scurry down the hall as the doorbell rings for a second time. I grab the first thing I see in my suitcase, a pair of boxers, and pull them on. My trousers are in the other bag. I rummage around for a shirt.

Sam emerges from her room wearing a terry-cloth robe and makes a beeline for the front door. She swings it open—and gapes at the people standing outside. "Mom? Dad? What in the world are you doing here?"

Oh bloody hell. Her parents are here.

And I'm half-naked.

Chapter Ten

Sam

My parents are standing in front of me, smiling, while I'm pretty sure Ben is behind me somewhere dressed in only a pair of boxer shorts. No, that won't make my parents suspicious at all. So what if I never mentioned having a boyfriend? Ben doesn't qualify for that title anyway, since we met less than twenty-four hours ago. But I so do not want to explain to my mom and dad why a half-naked Brit is standing in my living room.

Why did I open the door when he wasn't dressed yet? That man turns my brain to mush.

"Hi, Mom," I say while grinning like an idiot. "Hi, Dad."

They both squint at me.

Dad speaks first while pointing in the general direction of Ben. "Who's that? And why isn't he dressed?"

"Well, uh, see…" I'm off to a great start, stammering and gaping at my parents while my heart pounds. I glance over my shoulder at my British guest. At least he's got pants on now, but he's still shirtless. "That's my friend, Ben. We met yesterday when his car got stuck on the road, just down the hill from here."

"She rescued me," Ben says. He pulls on a T-shirt and saunters up beside me, offering his hand to my father. "Bennett Montague. It's a pleasure to meet you, sir."

"Chuck Lockhart." Dad shakes Ben's hand. "And this is my wife, Judy."

Ben shakes my mom's hand too.

"Um…" I say while I try to make my brain start working again. "Why don't you guys come inside? It's kind of chilly out there."

Dad looks at Ben, giving him a visual once over. His lips tighten, and he seems to be very interested in Ben's hair. Probably because it's wet. Well, Ben might've taken a shower. Wet hair doesn't automatically mean I was going down on Ben in the hot tub. Of course, I'm wearing a bathrobe, and my hair is damp too.

My cheeks get warm. Fabulous. Ben and I look like we just took a shower together. That's what my parents will think, I'm sure, since the Lockharts do not go nude in a hot tub, a swimming pool, or anywhere except the privacy of a bathroom.

I lead my parents into the living room.

And that's when I remember I left the box of condoms on the table beside the entrance to the hallway. Since I have no luck at all, my mom swerves her gaze in that direction while appraising the living room, and I can tell she sees the condoms.

Mom lifts her brows, then looks at me.

I hunch my shoulders.

She smiles and winks.

Whatever that means, I don't have a clue. But maybe she's telling me she doesn't think I'm a total slut and a complete moron for inviting a foreigner to stay in my home. Once they get to know Ben, I'm sure even my dad will like him. It's hard not to like Ben. I've never met another man as kind and smart and fun as Bennett Montague.

My parents sit down on the sofa while Ben and I take the armchairs.

And we sit here. In silence. For a long time.

Okay, it's probably a minute at most. But the seconds ticking by feel like hours.

Finally, my dad rests one ankle on the other knee and stares straight at Ben. "So, Mr. Montague, where are you from?"

"I live in England."

"What are you doing here in America?"

"Taking a holiday. I was supposed to spend Christmas at my mate Chance's house in Hartmoor, but the snowstorm waylaid me. Your daughter was kind enough to save me when my car died during the blizzard, and she gave me a place to stay until the roads are clear."

I suddenly realize one important fact. "How did you guys get here? The plow's broken, so the roads are still impassable."

"Not anymore," Dad says. "We got stuck at the airport all night, then we finally managed to get through to North Slipperton an hour ago. We heard the roads up here had just been reopened."

"That's right," Mom says. "We bumped into Wayne Hendley in town, and he told us the plow's been fixed and it's all clear."

My mind circles back to my original question, which no one has answered yet. "Okay, I get how you managed to drive here. But why are you guys here at all?"

"We couldn't leave our baby out here alone at Christmas," Mom says. Her gaze drifts to Ben, and I swear she ogles him. "If we'd known you had company, we would've called ahead. But your father thought it would be fun to surprise you."

My parents don't do surprise visits. So of course, the first time they ever do that turns out to be the day I have a half-naked man in my living room. Jeez, I'm an adult. I shouldn't care what my parents think. Sure, because nobody over the age of eighteen ever feels that way.

"Where are you and Dad staying?" I ask my mother.

"Here." She says that like I invited them to come for a surprise visit and knew they'd need a place to crash. "You have a guest bedroom."

"No, not anymore. I'm using the upstairs for storage. Removed the furniture and put it in storage in town."

"You what? Your grandfather always had a room for guests."

"Well, I..." Suddenly feel like a kid again, like I just got caught reading a dirty magazine under the covers. But I am not a child. Time to act like the adult I'm supposed to be. "This is my house now, and I needed the storage space. I'm sorry. You'll need to stay at the bed-and-breakfast in town."

"Can't," Dad says. "We drove past it coming through town, and the sign said 'no vacancy.' But don't worry. We'll drive back into good old North Slipperton and buy us an air mattress. I'm sure that store has them."

This is just perfect. I finally meet a nice guy who I want to have sex with all day and all night, and my parents show up to wreck my naughty holiday. Don't get me wrong, I'm happy to see Mom and Dad. The timing sucks, that's all.

"Are you guys hungry?" I ask. "I could make sandwiches for you."

"No, sweetie, we're fine," Mom says. "I think your father and I should go straight back to town to get that air mattress."

"I'd offer you the sofa bed, but that's where Ben sleeps." Okay, maybe I slipped that bit of info into the conversation strictly so my parents will get the idea that I'm not sleeping with Ben. Sure, I've gotten naked with him. But we're not sleeping together. "I should at least go with you to the Discount Depot."

"No, no, we don't want to be a bother," Mom says. "You and Ben stay here. Chuck, let's get going so we can be back before sunset."

"Sounds like a plan," Dad says as he stands up. He squints at Ben and speaks in a growly tone. "I got my eye on you, Brit boy. If you hurt my daughter, I'll gut you like a carp and have you for dinner."

Ben just stares at my father.

Dad bursts out laughing and points at Ben. "I had you, didn't I?"

"Yes, you did," Ben says with a nervous laugh. "You had me going for a minute, Mr. Lockhart."

"Call me Chuck." Dad grabs Mom's hand, urging her to rise. "Shake a leg, Judy. Time's a-wasting."

Ben and I follow my parents to the front door and watch them get into their car. As they drive off, I shut the door and lean back against it.

"I am so sorry," I tell Ben. "My dad isn't usually like that."

"So fish-related death threats aren't a common occurrence in your family."

"No. I think my parents are just confused by the fact I have a stranger living with me. I've never lived with anyone except my family."

"Really?" Ben leans his shoulder against the door beside me. "Chuck did have me going for a second or two, but I like that he wants to torment me with fish humor."

"Why would you like that?"

"Because I think it means he likes me. Don't you?"

I need to consider that suggestion for a few seconds. "Maybe that's what it means. My dad hasn't had much opportunity to torment my boyfriends since I rarely introduced any of them to my parents."

"But why not? You seem close with your mum and dad."

"Sure, I am. But I've never had much luck with men. It's embarrassing to introduce a guy to my parents, then have to tell them two weeks later that the jerk dumped me for a girl with breast implants the size of beach balls."

He studies me for a moment, searching my face with his gaze. "You've dated the wrong sort of men."

"I know. But it's nearly impossible to find a decent guy these days." I bite the inside of my lip as I look at Ben. "Then one just fell into my lap."

"Never been happier to get stranded in a blizzard."

"Do you, um, have to go home right away?"

He leans closer, gazing straight into my eyes. "I was hoping you'd ask me that. The answer is yes, but I don't give a toss. Doing my duty has only made me miserable."

"What duty are you talking about? I thought you were a massage therapist, but you make it sound like you're in the military or something."

"No, it's nothing like that." He sighs and rubs his eyes with his thumb and forefinger. "I suppose it's time I told you the truth about me."

Oh great. Is he married? Or maybe he's actually gay. Both of those scenarios have happened to me, so I'm not just being paranoid. But we've had plenty of sizzling-hot sex, which seems to rule out option two. That leaves option one. He must be married. With half a dozen adorable little British kids. He hasn't wanted to talk about his family much, and he's been cagey about where he's from, always saying he lives in England. That's not the same as being *from* there.

Yeah, he must be married. I'm an adulteress.

Ben pushes away from the door, facing me, though he bows his head and scratches his scalp. "I want to stay here with you and your parents for Christmas, if you want me around for that long. But I, ah…need to tell you the truth about me first."

Yep, now I'm sure he's not only married, but he probably has three wives in various places around the world with dozens of adorable little British babies.

"Bloody hell," he moans. "It shouldn't be this hard to tell the truth."

"Just spit it out." Before I turn into a nervous wreck, thanks to my fantasies of his bigamist lifestyle.

He straightens, lifts his chin, and looks straight at me. "I am Bennett Worthington Montague, crown prince of Mithoria."

My jaw drops.

Chapter Eleven

Ben

Samantha Lockhart is gaping at me like I've just told her I'm an alien from Jupiter and I want to impregnate her with my lizard spawn. I've seen all sorts of reactions when I tell people who I am, the few times I've done that, but never has anyone stared at me with such complete shock. How will her parents react? If Sam can't deal with the truth, I shouldn't expect her parents to be happy about it either. They will probably think I'm delusional. The fact that no one has ever heard of Mithoria doesn't help my case.

I expect to be carted away in a straitjacket any minute now.

"Are you all right?" I ask.

Sam blinks several times, her lids fluttering. "Huh? Oh, yeah, of course. I'm perfectly fine. What did you just say you are?"

"The crown prince of Mithoria."

"Mith-what?"

I reach out to touch her arm, but pull my hand away. "Mithoria. It's a tiny principality on a tiny island that no one has ever heard of."

"But I thought you were British."

And here comes the part where I try to explain my nationality and my heritage. It always confuses people. "I am British. I was born in the UK and went to boarding school there, not to mention university. I've spent more time in England than I have in Mithoria. But I have dual citizenship. So I am both British and Mithorian."

"Oh. Sure. That makes sense." She says that as if it makes no sense at all.

Yeah, that's the usual response.

"I realize this is a big shock," I say, shoving my hands into my trouser pockets. "I should've told you sooner, but I hadn't planned to stay any longer than necessary. Now I want to spend more time with you and your parents. A normal family Christmas sounds like the perfect holiday to me since this time of year can get… Well, let's just say there's far too much pageantry involved in a Mithorian Christmas."

"But don't you want to be with your family? Are they so awful?"

"Not awful." I wince as I try to figure out how to explain. "My father is Prince Leighton of Mithoria, and he rules over the country with the help of the parliament. My mother, Princess Olivia, rules alongside him. My younger sister, Stephanie, has more of an honorary role, but she loves all the royal bollocks." I try not to twist my mouth up, but I can't help it. "As for me, I'm expected to marry a proper aristocratic lady."

"So why are you here instead of at home courting those ladies? I'm anything but proper. I mean, we had sex in a restaurant."

"And I loved that. I love everything we do together." I clasp her hand. "Could we sit down on the sofa? Talking about all this rubbish makes me need to rest my bum."

"Sure." She smiles. "Can't have that fine bum getting sore."

Once we've sat down, I sink back into the sofa and let my head fall onto the cushion. "Until a week ago, I was in Mithoria doing my royal duty. I let my mother parade aristocratic girls in front of me, and I tried to at least tolerate, if not actually like, at least one of them. I couldn't do it. They're a bunch of scheming shrews who lust after my title and the power they'll have once I become prince of Mithoria. Right now, I'm just a crown prince. But when my father dies, I will take over."

"You sound like you're not happy about that."

I did sound rather pathetic, didn't I? Bugger me. "Maybe I'm not happy about marrying a nasty girl and hoping I might grow to tolerate her, eventually. Love is out of the question. But my mother doesn't see it that way. She married my father when they barely knew each other, and love came later." I shake my head. "But I will never grow to care for any of those girls. The last one suggested I shag her so I could see that we're sexually compatible. I'd rather shag a porcupine."

"Ouch. That girl must've been a piece of work."

"They all are. That's why I ran away."

Sam turns toward me and tucks her feet under her. "You ran away to New Hampshire. That's kind of a weird choice for a vacation spot when you're a British Mithorian. Have you ever been to America before?"

"No. My mates helped me escape from England before my mother showed up. Chance Dixon's house seemed like the perfect place to hide while I figure out what to do."

"Can a crown prince decide not to be one? Can you abdicate or whatever?"

"Not sure." I scrub my hands over my face and groan. "I don't want to upset my family or let my country down. But I can't live that way anymore. I love my life in England."

"Well, maybe you should just have fun here in New Hampshire and worry about the rest later." She brushes her fingers through my hair, grazing my scalp with every pass. "You seem super stressed about all this. I'm thinking you need a vacation. Lucky for you, I have a sofa bed waiting for you and lots of ideas for fun things we can do for the holidays."

"You are an angel, Sam."

She kisses my cheek. "I don't want you to leave yet, that's all. Does my ulterior motive bother you?"

"Not in the least. Have as many ulterior motives as you like."

"Well, I do have one other secret reason for wanting to keep you around." She places her mouth over my ear and whispers, "I love shagging you."

"And I love getting a leg over with you."

She wraps her tongue around my earlobe while she slides her hand up my thigh.

"Not sure we should be doing this," I say. "Your parents will be back soon. We probably shouldn't have sex at all while they're here."

"Didn't you ever sneak into a girl's room in the dead of night?"

"No, I couldn't. At boarding school, there were only boys. And in Mithoria, the castle had guards everywhere, so I couldn't sneak out."

Sam sits back, studying me with her lips puckered. After a moment, she smiles and pats my cheek. "Then you've got a lot of naughtiness to make up for."

"I've done that already, with you. Here on the sofa bed last night, in the restaurant today, and in the hot tub earlier."

"Oh, but you've got a lifetime's worth of bad behavior to catch up on." She slides over to straddle my lap. "Tonight, I want you to sneak into my bedroom and have your way with me."

"Your father wants to gut me like a fish."

"He was joking." She reaches down to lay her palm over my cock. "Besides, the whole point of being naughty is to toss all the rules out the window, and damn the consequences."

I pretend I'm considering the repercussions of doing what she suggests. Then I grasp her arse. "All right. I'm in. Let's be irresponsible."

She throws her hands up and whoops.

And I flip us both over so we're lying lengthwise on the sofa with me on top. "Let's start right now."

Her smile fades. "I almost forgot. We need to get the upstairs ready for my parents."

"Ah, well. I guess misbehaving can wait a little longer."

We head upstairs to what looks like an attic. It has a ceiling that slants low overhead as if it's following the pitch of the roof. Sam has a lot of boxes stacked inside this space, and it takes us a while to carry them downstairs and stow them in the walk-in closet in her bedroom. When we run out of space there, we stack the remaining boxes up against the wall in the upstairs room. It does have a small closet, but we have to leave that one empty for her parents to use. Now it's time to clean the room. A good sweeping-out sounds like enough to me, but Sam insists we have to sweep and mop the floors, not to mention cleaning the windows. We've left the little table that was in here where we found it. Her parents can use it as a nightstand.

Finally done with our task, we collapse onto the sofa together. Sam cuddles up to me, and I curl an arm around her shoulders.

The front door swings open. Chuck and Judy barrel into the house carrying multiple bags that have the names of various shops on them.

Sam and I get up to greet them.

The woman who encouraged me to be naughty gapes at the bags her parents are holding. "I thought you were just going into town to buy an air mattress."

"We bought more food too. I bet your cupboards are almost bare."

"Not almost bare. I don't have enough food for a small army, though, like you guys seem to have."

While Chuck and Judy set down their bags, he says, "We'll need to make more trips to town. Maybe even go to the big city. It's Christmastime, after all, which means lots of presents."

"Please don't go overboard," Sam says. "I was hoping for a quiet Christmas."

Judy waves a hand in a dismissive gesture. "Oh please. Nobody wants a subdued holiday. People say that, but what they mean is they don't want to be too much trouble. We're family. It's our job to make sure you overdo Christmas."

Sam glances at me like she wants me to agree with her "quiet Christmas" idea. But I can't lie. What her parents have suggested sounds like fun. Should I tell them who I am? Well, I suppose it's the right thing to do since I'm having sex with their daughter.

"Your plan sounds brilliant," I say. "But I should tell you about me first. Sam already knows, and I don't want to keep secrets from you lot. You've been very kind to me."

I've decided to pretend Chuck never suggested he might gut me like a carp.

"Are you an ex-con?" Chuck asks. "Whether we're okay with that depends on what you did."

"No, I'm not a criminal." I glance at Sam, who gives me an encouraging smile. Then I face her parents. "I'm the crown prince of Mithoria. That's a principality in the middle of the Atlantic Ocean."

Chuck stares at me blankly for a moment, then he starts laughing. "Good one, kid."

"I'm not joking. It's true. My father is Prince Leighton, and my mother is Princess Olivia."

Judy just stares at me.

Chuck brings out his mobile and types on its screen. Squinting, he scrolls through something. Then his brows lift, and he swings his gaze to me. "You're not kidding. I just looked you up online."

Sam believed me without the aid of the internet, but I can understand why her father needed confirmation. He's looking out for his daughter. Chuck must have found the official Mithoria website since I'm not exactly famous to the majority of the world. Paparazzi don't follow me around in hopes of getting a juicy picture. Nobody knows about Mithoria unless they live there or meet someone who does. We're just not that important.

"What's a prince doing in New Hampshire?" Chuck asks. "Wouldn't you rather go for a ski vacation in the Swiss Alps?"

"I hate skiing. And besides, I wanted to get away from all that rubbish."

"What 'rubbish' is that?"

Sam's father doesn't sound annoyed or suspicious. No, he's just asking the sort of questions any parent might want to know the answers to when he finds a stranger sharing his daughter's house. If I were in his place, I'm sure I'd do the same thing.

"Why don't we all sit down?" I say. "Giving you the answers you want will take a while."

"You're not old enough to have a life story so long we need to sit down for it."

Chuck is smirking while he says that, which I decide means he's teasing me. That's a good sign, isn't it? He must not think I'm an arse after all.

I tell them all about me while Chuck and Judy sit on the sofa and Sam and I take separate armchairs, just the way we'd sat earlier. I leave out the boring bits that won't tell them anything about who I am, but I feel like I do need to share my life story with them. Maybe I've only known Sam for twenty-four hours or thereabouts, but I already know I want to see where this thing between us might go. That means getting to know each other, which also means letting her parents get to know me too. I tell them the abridged version of my life, from boarding school to university to my mother summoning me home for the first time.

I hadn't wanted to go back to Mithoria after university. In England, I was just another bloke. People liked me or not based on who I am, not the title I bear. Everyone at boarding school had known about me, but I became just another student at university. That's where I met Reese Dixon, Chance's youngest brother, and everything snowballed after that. I met Reese's brothers, then the Hunters too. Nick and Richard are much older than I am, but we became good friends anyway.

Even when I told them about myself, they treated me like just another member of their circle of mates.

"What did you study in college?" Judy asks.

"I, uh, well…" Stammering is not my favorite way to engage in conversation, but I worry that Sam's parents will think I'm a loser when I tell them everything. *Take a deep breath and just do it.* "I have a law degree."

"You're a lawyer, eh?" Chuck says. "Not sure how I feel about that."

"No, I'm not a lawyer. I earned my qualifying law degree, but I never became a solicitor."

I haven't even told Sam about that yet. She doesn't look shocked or annoyed. She wears a sweet, soft smile as she watches me and listens to my story.

"A solicitor is a lawyer," I explain. "At any rate, I only studied law because my parents expected me to. I tried very hard to like the law, but I just couldn't commit my life to it. My parents were disappointed."

Chuck narrows his gaze on me, though he's not quite squinting. "What do you do for a living, Ben?"

"I'm a massage therapist at a day spa in Cockshire, England."

Judy's brows shoot up, then she smiles slyly. "Cockshire? That's where you live? Sounds like you work at an adults-only spa."

Does Sam's mother have a dirty mind? Sure seems as if she does. Like mother like daughter.

"It's just a normal day spa," I say. "No idea why the town is called Cockshire, but I did not name the place. Most of my clients are recovering from injuries, and what I do is more like physical therapy than a traditional massage."

"Maybe you can help me out," Chuck says. "I keep hurting my back."

"I'd be happy to give you a massage. Back pain is the most frequent reason our clients at Nick's Nirvana give for wanting a treatment."

"Nick's Nirvana?" Judy says. She gives me another sly smile. "And you say it's just a regular old spa."

"My mate Nick Hunter owns the place. He thought using nirvana in the name would make it sound more relaxing and welcoming."

"I was teasing you, dear. Of course I don't think you work at a brothel."

Nick had been accused of that not long ago, by a nasty woman who wanted to punish him for refusing to give her a "special" massage. But Sam's parents don't need to hear about that.

"If you're the crown prince," Chuck says, "shouldn't you be in Mith-whatsit instead of in England or America?"

"My mother wanted me to go back to Mithoria after university, but I told her I needed to find out what the real world was like before I committed to the royal lifestyle." I sit forward, elbows on my knees, and stare down at the wood floor. "Honestly, I knew even then that I didn't want to become the future ruler of Mithoria. It's just not the kind of life I want."

"Do you have a choice?" Sam asks.

I turn my head slightly to look at her, wondering if she wants me to stay for longer than a couple of weeks. I want that. But after hearing all about me, I wouldn't blame her if she'd rather not get involved with me.

"According to my mother," I say, "I don't have a choice. It's my duty, and no respectable crown prince shirks his responsibilities."

"Will you eventually become the ruler of Mithoria?"

"Only when my father dies. Right now, I'm essentially a figurehead they trot out at official functions." I slump backward into my chair and sigh. "A few months back, my mother ordered me to go home and find a suitable wife."

Chuck does squint at me this time. "So why are you here with my daughter? If you're looking for a wife back home?"

"Because I'm not looking for a wife in Mithoria. I've tried, but the only women my mother thinks are suitable don't suit me. They're aristocrats of proper breeding, but they're bloody awful human beings." I pause to calm myself before I go on. The last thing I want to do is sound like a whingeing arse. "Look, I know I've had every advantage, and I'm not saying my life has been harder than anyone else's. All I know is that marrying a woman I don't love, don't even know, is not how I want to live."

"What do you want?" Sam asks.

I meet her gaze, and I don't care that her parents are listening. "To stay here with you and find out what we could have together, that's what I want. But I understand if you don't want that. Now you know the whole story of me. I ran away from Mithoria because I couldn't stand the 'find Ben a princess' bollocks. I ran away, which means I'm a bloody coward."

Chapter Twelve

Sam

Ben thinks he's a coward. Okay, I get why he feels that way. Now that I've heard his story, I understand why he'd been reluctant to tell me about his family and his life back home. But I think "home" to him means Cockshire, not Mithoria. Being the crown prince isn't his real life, not anymore. He loves his job and his friends, and I can understand why he ran away from Mithoria. I would never want someone else to choose my spouse for me. How can Ben's mother do that to him? Why doesn't his dad intervene? Well, maybe he agrees with his wife that Ben shouldn't have a choice.

Maybe this whatever-it-is between me and Ben won't work out, but I want to give us a chance. I don't want him to leave, not yet.

"You ran away?" Dad says to Ben. "Did you even tell your parents where you went?"

"No, I, uh…" Ben squirms in his chair while wincing slightly. "It's complicated. My mother has a habit of summoning me back to Mithoria, whether I want to go or not. She didn't come herself to retrieve me, though. She sends her minions."

"Minions?" I say. "That sounds awful."

"I didn't mean it that way. Mum doesn't like England, so she would send one of the palace guards to come get me."

"How many times did that happen?"

"Three times. Before, I could always negotiate with my mother for more time in England, and I did promise I'd try to find a wife, eventually." He covers his face with his hands and groans. Then he lowers his hands. "This time, I had to do it. But every girl Mum introduced me to was greedy and hungry for a title, not interested in me. I can't imagine spending the rest of my life with a girl like that. Mum insists I'll grow to love my wife, but I can't see that happening with any of the rich girls she brought to me."

"You make it sound like she served them up on a platter."

"It felt that way."

Mom clears her throat. "Maybe we should give you two some time alone to talk about all of this. Chuck, let's get our air mattress set up."

"Ben and I should help you," I say.

"We might be older than you two, but we aren't decrepit yet. Dad and I will manage."

My parents grab two of their shopping bags and head upstairs.

Ben sits there slumped in his chair, head down, looking so defeated that I want to hug him. Well, why shouldn't I? We've had sex, for heaven's sake. That gives me the right to comfort him. So I walk over to his chair and settle my butt on his lap, then loop my arms around his neck.

"What are you doing?" he asks, lifting his head.

"You need a cuddle. I can tell."

"I just told you I'm a ruddy coward who ran away from home rather than dealing with my problems."

"That's not what I heard." I nuzzle his cheek. "Everything you said told me that you're lonely and miserable in Mithoria. You love your life in England, and you don't want to marry some rich girl just to be proper. Running away might not have been the best choice, but I understand why you did it."

"I did leave a note. But that's childish too."

"You are not childish. You're struggling to find your way, that's all."

He tips his head to the side while studying me. "Why do you believe the best of me? I've told you I'm a spoiled rich boy who doesn't appreciate everything my family provides for me."

"Why do you keep trying to convince me you're nothing but an ungrateful spoiled brat?"

"I shouldn't have run away. I guess I'm feeling guilty about that."

"You could call your parents to apologize. Explain the situation to them. They might be more understanding than you think."

"Dad is much easier to talk to than Mum. She takes her royal duties very seriously."

"That's admirable. But she shouldn't force you to live the way she does."

"I'm the crown prince. When my father dies, I'm expected to take over."

Maybe that's true, but I have to ask a question. "Can't your sister become the crown princess or something? Take over in your place?"

He screws up his mouth. "Mithoria has always had a prince as ruler, and I'm the eldest, anyway. Not sure if the law allows a princess to take on that role. Never thought about it, actually. I doubt my mother would go for that, though."

It's time we get off the topic of his home country and his mother. Ben came to America for a vacation, to have fun and enjoy being a normal guy. Despite his title and his pedigree, Ben seems like just that—an average guy.

"Tell you what," I say. "Let's forget about all that stuff and just enjoy Christmas together."

"Sounds perfect. I know I'll need to deal with my mother eventually, but I'd love to relax and have a good time with you and your family."

"Let's just hope my brother and his family don't show up too. You'll be sleeping in the hot tub then."

He stares at me. "You don't think they would actually show up here, do you?"

"Probably not. Even if they do, you'll like them and they'll like you. Guaranteed."

Ben slips his arms around me, clasping his hands over my hip. "I feel better when I'm with you, like none of that other rubbish matters."

"From now until Christmas, don't worry about anything except having fun." I hesitate, but then add, "Though maybe you should let your family know you're okay. Don't have to tell them exactly where you are."

"I texted my sister just after I left the airport on my ill-fated journey to Hartmoor. She would've told Mum and Dad. They know I'm in America, staying at a friend's house, but not the precise location."

"Good. Now that we've settled all that, let's do something fun with my parents. They'd love to get to know you better, and so would I."

He nods with feigned seriousness. "Ah, the interrogation is about to begin in earnest."

I poke him in the belly. "Better not mock the woman who's giving you a place to sleep and awesome sex."

"Am I mocking you? Thought I was being facetious instead."

Footsteps on the stairs catch our attention, and we both realize my parents are coming back. So I jump off Ben's lap, standing up. He's just pushing up out of his chair when my parents reach the living room.

"We were trying to think of something fun to do," I say. "Something we can all do together."

"I've got an idea," Dad says, rubbing his hands together. "Let's play games."

Ben and I exchange looks that I think mean we're both thinking the same thing. Games? Yeah, we played one of those earlier, but it involved stripping. No, I don't think I'll mention that to my father.

Dad walks up to Ben and slaps his arm. "Ever play war, kid?"

Ben's forehead crinkles. "War?"

"The card game. Don't they have that in England?"

"Not sure. I've never heard of it, but I'm hardly an expert on card games."

"You'll like it." Dad slaps Ben's arm again. "It's easy to play. I'll show you how."

I sidle up to Ben, slipping my arm around his. "It's strictly a game of chance. No strategy involved. But it's actually lots of fun, especially the way my family plays it."

"All right," Ben says. "I'm in."

"Terrific!" Dad almost shouts.

Why my father is so happy that Ben will play a card game with him, I have no idea. I hope it means Dad likes Ben, because I like him a whole lot.

But he's a crown prince from another country. Maybe I shouldn't get too attached to him, since I doubt his mother would ever approve of me, but I can't help it. Ben is the nicest guy I've ever met. Could we find a way to be together even without his family's consent? Not sure I want to be the wedge that drives them apart, but I'm also positive I don't belong in his world.

I'm being a worrywart. Since I just met Ben, it's way too soon to fret over our star-crossed relationship.

We sit down at the dining room table to play war. Since the "dining room" is just an open space beside the living room, I'm not sure it actually counts as a separate space. The round maple-wood table fits four chairs nicely, so we seat ourselves around it and put the deck of cards on the tabletop. Only two players can participate at one time. Dad and Ben go first.

"It's real simple," Dad says. "We each take half the deck and place it face down. Then we both lay a card down at the same time, face up. Whoever gets the highest card wins the hand. We do that over and over until one of us has all the cards."

"Sounds easy enough," Ben says. "Let's go."

My father fake-squints at Ben. "How fast can you flip a card, kid?"

Ben fake-squints right back at my dad. "As fast as you can. Maybe even faster."

Dad counts out the cards, separating them into two stacks of twenty-six each. He hands one stack to Ben. Then my father rests one finger on his cards and affects an even squintier fake-squint. "Ready, kid?"

Ben hunches forward slightly, his finger on his stack of cards, and stares intently at my dad. "Oh yes, I'm ready."

"Let's see what kind of quickdraw you are."

Jeez, he's making it sound like this is a duel to the death at high noon with six-shooters. Well, at least they're having fun.

Dad flips his first card.

And Ben flips his over at almost the same instant.

My father wins that hand, but as the game progresses, they keep flipping cards faster and Ben gains some ground. Then they both hit the same card at the same time.

"You know what this means," Dad says, doing that squinty thing again. "It's war."

"I thought we were already playing war," Ben says. "Did I miss something?"

"Here's how it works. If we both flip the same card at the same time, it's war. Now we both lay down two extra cards, one face up and one face down. Whoever has the highest card takes all six."

"What do you mean all six?"

"All the cards we set down in war. That means the original two and the four new ones. Six total."

"Oh, I get it. Let's go to war, then."

They do just that, and Ben wins the hand. They keep playing at lightning speed, pausing only when they hit war, which happens twice more. By the end of the game, only one player has all fifty-two cards.

Ben throws his hands up and grins. "I won the war!"

Dad grins too. "Sure did. You flip cards almost as fast as I do. Nice job, kid."

"Thank you, Chuck. I haven't had this much fun playing a game in a long time."

"Didn't your family ever play games?"

"We did, when I was a boy. But our lifestyle and responsibilities kept us from playing as much as we would've liked."

"Right. Being royalty probably gets a little stifling sometimes, hey?"

Ben hunches his shoulders and gazes down at the tabletop. "I would never claim my life is harder than anyone else's. I've had all the advantages—money, connections, privilege. But sometimes I do wish I were just an average bloke."

I lay a hand on his arm. "You *are* a normal guy, Ben. Your title and money don't change that."

"Thank you, Sam. But I know my status makes a lot of people uncomfortable, which is why I don't tell everyone who I am."

My dad leans back in his chair, eying Ben with a curious expression. "Hope you won't take this the wrong way, but if you're rich, why do you work at a day spa? I mean, why do you take money for working there?"

"I might be technically wealthy, but I don't currently have access to my trust fund. My mother cut me off when I announced I wanted to stay in England and become a massage therapist."

"She cut you off?" I say, my fingers tightening a smidgen on his arm. "That's awful."

"Mum isn't a horrible person. She was trying to convince me to do my duty. I think she honestly believed that cutting me off would encourage me to go home and get married." He lifts his head and gives me a rueful little smile. "Instead, it helped me realize that life is more than being the figurehead of a tiny principality no one has ever heard of. I love the life I've made for myself, and I don't want to go back to the 'find a princess' rubbish."

Dad scrutinizes Ben. "Don't you want to rule Mith-whatsit?"

"No, I don't. Mithoria is a nice enough place, but I'd much rather be in Cockshire." He glances at me and smiles. "Or in North Slipperton."

I feel warm all over when he looks at me that way, like he wants to spend forever right here with me in this cabin. Maybe I'm starting to wish for that too. It's crazy since we just met, but we'll have almost two full weeks to figure out how we feel about each other.

Dad sits up straight and shuffles the deck of cards. "What say we watch the ladies duke it out in war?"

"Absolutely," Ben says with a grin. "Let's see if they can flip cards as fast as we do."

Mom and I play our round of war, and she wins. I don't care, though. I'm not a super competitive person, and besides, this is just for fun. Mom and Dad play each other next. She out-flips him time and again, but he doesn't care. They razz each other and pretend to cheat, just so they can pretend to be offended. Yeah, my family is kind of weird, but I love them.

When Ben and I face off in war, I win. Ben asks me what I want as my prize, and I lean in to whisper in his ear so no one else will hear what I say. "Some playtime in the hot tub, just the two of us. No interruptions."

He smirks.

Not sure if we can find that uninterrupted alone time, what with my parents on the premises. We can try, though. And if all else fails, Ben can sneak into my bedroom late at night for under-the-sheets playtime. Even while I plan what fun things we can all do together for the holidays, I keep wondering about that one thing.

Should I really date a crown prince?

Chapter Thirteen

Ben

Sam and I don't get that naked playtime in the hot tub after all, not that day or the next, but neither of us minds. We enjoy spending time with her parents, playing all sorts of board games and card games, not to mention going for snowy nature walks and taking trips into the village of North Slipperton. I keep trying to think of a gift I can buy for Sam for Christmas, but I haven't come up with the perfect idea yet.

We all take turns cooking meals too. I'm starting to feel like I've become a member of the Lockhart family, and they definitely treat me that way. Every time I think about that, I remember my family. Maybe I should go home to deal with my problems, but not yet. I need more time to decide what to do, or rather, how to convince my mother to let me lead my own life.

On my third day in New Hampshire, I finally retrieve my car from where it broke down on the road. When I'd asked Sam on day two whether we should get my car yet, she told me not to worry about that because "this isn't London, it's the backwoods of New Hampshire." Apparently, that means nobody will crash into the vehicle I hired. I took her word for that.

A tow truck hauls the car away to a repair shop in North Slipperton, and Sam and I ride back to the cabin on her snowmobile. We could've driven her car, but she loves to go very fast and cut across areas where there are no roads. The fact that my car doesn't work gives me another excuse to stay here. Do I need an excuse? I'm an adult and can do whatever I want, but I know my mother won't agree with that statement.

Chuck teaches me how to change a flat tire, though his car doesn't have a flat. He shows me how it's done anyway, in case I ever get myself into trouble on the road again. I remind him it wasn't a tire that did me in, but he just smiles and slaps my arm. I've decided that means he likes me. Knowing how to fix a flat is a useful skill, so I'm glad Chuck showed me that. I would offer to teach him how to give a massage, but that seems sort of…weird. No, I don't think I'll make that offer. Maybe I should suggest it to Sam instead.

Over the next several days, I don't get much time alone with her. It's all right, though. I haven't had this much fun in ages, and Sam's parents are a big part of the reason I'm feeling so good. I love my family, but Christmas back home has never been relaxed. It's a formal occasion with formal clothes and formal meals and all that "proper" rubbish. When I mention that to Sam, she seems confused.

"Have you never experienced a normal, old-fashioned Christmas?" she asks. "You've been living in England, so I figured you went to a friend's house for the holidays."

"No, I always went home to Mithoria like a good little boy. This is the first time in my life when I've had a normal Christmas. Or at least what most people think that means."

"For you, normal is stuffy and structured."

"Ah…yes. I'm grateful for all the advantages I've had, but it's nice not to worry about whether my collar is starched properly or if my shoes are polished to a blinding shine."

"Well, I'm definitely glad you ditched the formal Christmas for a down-home one with me."

Sam and I are sitting on the sofa, and we are at last alone. Chuck and Judy went into town to hunt for more gifts. Honestly, I don't know how those two have the energy for all the shopping they do. They invited me and Sam to go with them so we could have lunch at the Crab Cottage, but we opted to stay home. Every time anyone mentions that restaurant, I think I start to blush. What we did there… I can't believe I had sex in a public place. But I'd love to do it again.

Just not with her parents sitting across the table from us.

"Since we're alone," I say, slipping my arm around her shoulders, "why don't we finish what we started in the hot tub the other day."

"Ooh, I'd love that." She snuggles closer to me. "I've been hoping we'd get a chance to play in the hot tub again."

"Why don't you go out and get the jets bubbling while I grab what we'll need?"

"I hope you mean condoms."

"Yes." I raise my brows. "Condoms plural? How many do you think we'll need?"

"Depends on how long my parents are gone." She hops up and grabs my hands, urging me to get up too. "Get a move on, Ben. Don't want to lose our window of opportunity."

I rise and slap her arse. "Get a move on, Sam."

When I turn to walk away, she smacks my arse.

I glance back at her. "What was that for? I *am* getting a move on."

"Sorry, couldn't help myself. Your fine ass always makes me want to slap it or pinch it."

Her adorably sexy smile makes me want to throw her down on the sofa and start our naked fun right here and now. But I desperately need to shag her in the hot tub, so I restrain myself and hurry into her bedroom, where I've stashed my suitcases. Everyone kept tripping over them in the living room. I catch a glimpse of Sam racing past the doorway, heading for the porch and the hot tub. She's still dressed, but I imagine she wants to have her clothes out there with us in case her parents come home early.

I grab the box of condoms and rush after her.

By the time I get out onto the porch, Sam is in the hot tub—naked, with the jets bubbling all around her, making her tits float up and her hair fan out around her. She lies mostly submerged, with only her head out of the water. All of her creamy skin is on display.

I set the box of condoms on the ledge that surrounds the tub. Then I strip and jump in with her.

Water splashes up, making her laugh.

"Never done this in the water before," I say. "How should we proceed?"

"Proceed?" She laughs again. "You are so cute when you talk that way. Proceed to fuck me, that's how you do it."

"Right. Sorry."

"Do all Brits say 'sorry' every other word?"

"I think so. Haven't met all the other Brits, though, so I can't swear to that."

"You can't? Darn, I was planning to make you put one hand on a sex manual and raise your other hand to swear on the god of orgasms that all Brits use that word every three seconds."

It's my turn to laugh. "What does sex have to do with saying 'sorry'?"

"Nothing." She crooks a finger at me. "Get over here, Bennett Worthington Montague, and shag me like there's no tomorrow."

"There had better be a tomorrow, because I've got plans for all the things I want to do to your body from now until Christmas."

"Get on with it, then. Sheesh. You're jabbering instead of screwing me."

"Sorry."

Naturally, she laughs yet again. Because I said that word she thinks is so cute and hilarious.

I grab a condom and tear open the pack, but I run into a slight problem with getting it on my cock. This is the first time I've ever tried to shag a woman in a hot tub and the first time I've tried to put on a condom underwater. Turns out that's not so easy. The bloody jets keep pulling the condom out of my fingers, and the ruddy thing floats to the surface.

Sam is giggling now. She's the adorable one, with her cheeks dimpled and her eyes sparkling.

I give up and hoist myself onto the ledge with my arse balanced on it and finally get the damn condom on.

"Are you ready now?" Sam asks, while clearly trying not to smirk or laugh at me.

"Yes, I am ready." I slide off the ledge into the water, without splashing this time. "Time for hot tub sex."

"Ooh, yes please."

I pull her into my arms and kiss her, running my hands up and down her back while our tongues collide and her breasts get mashed between our bodies. Sam makes the sexiest little grunting noises while we devour each other, and when she grasps my arse, I groan into her mouth. She pushes her other hand into my hair, tunneling her fingers through it while she spreads her legs for me.

With my mouth still sealed over hers, I grasp her hips and pull her toward me while I thrust into her. Or I try to. But the motion of our bodies makes the water move too, and I have trouble, ah, hitting the target. So I back her up to the tub's wall, and grasp her hips again. But this time, I don't try to pull her into me. I thrust into her in one swift stroke, pinning her to the tub and sinking in deep as the warmth of her body surrounds my cock. She's hotter than the water, and the way her flesh conforms to my length feels so good that I never want to give up the sensation, even while I pull back and thrust into her again, starting a slow and steady rhythm.

Sam throws her head back and moans. "Oh God, Ben, I love to feel you inside me."

"I love it too." While the water bubbles and splashes around us, I grip the tub's rim at either side of her and thrust even harder, my pace quickening with every stroke. "Fucking you feels better than anything."

A surprised cry bursts out of her when I begin to pound into her, crushing her body to the tub wall and making little tidal waves crash over us and spill over the rim. I don't care that we're making a mess on the porch. It's only water, and she's got ice melt on hand.

Can't believe I'm thinking about that right now.

"Wrap your legs around me," I say, though I can barely speak and my voice sounds as rough as sandpaper.

She doesn't hesitate. Sam lashes her thighs around my hips and wraps her arms around my neck.

I stand up. Water sluices off our bodies while only my calves and knees are still submerged. I grasp her arse with both hands and start thrusting again. Sam bounces in my arms, her tits bouncing too, and clings to me while she buries her face against my neck and cries out every time I punch into her. No more sweet and gentle Bennett Montague. I lunge into her over and over, hard and fast, grunting and gasping as the sounds of our bodies colliding fill the air and echo off the trees.

She comes first, her body clenching me so many times that I can't stop myself from going off too. A sensation like electricity rockets down my spine and straight into my cock, setting off an unstoppable volley of spasms that rips through me so fast I can't breathe.

Then it's over. We're both panting while she still grips me with her arms and legs and I keep hold of her arse. Breathing isn't possible right now. I manage to gasp, but it takes a moment before I can achieve anything resembling normal respiration.

Sam goes limp in my arms. "Thank you, Ben. That was amazing."

"Thank *you*, Sam. I'm so glad my car broke down and stranded me near your house."

"Me too."

"Should we relax in the hot tub now?"

"Yes, please."

I set her down on her feet in the tub.

And a car door slams out front.

Samantha Lockhart leaps out of the hot tub, her eyes so wide I think they might pop out of their sockets. "Get dressed, Ben, quick. My parents are home."

Well, at least I got to shag her first.

<h1 style="text-align:center">Chapter Fourteen</h1>

Sam

I have never gotten dressed so fast in my entire life. Once I'm all covered up, I suffer a brief moment of panic about whether I got my clothes on the right way. But yes, it's all in the proper place. No inside-out shirt or panties lying on the porch boards at my feet.

Whew.

Ben gets dressed too, though he doesn't rush the way I did. He quickly pulls on his boxers, jeans, and T-shirt while managing to seem relaxed, not semi-panicked like me. Men are so lucky that they don't need to deal with bra clasps every morning when they get up—or after a steamy interlude in a hot tub. I succeeded in drying myself off just enough that my clothes don't stick my skin, but my hair is still wet.

We trot into the house and reach the front door just as my parents walk through it.

I don't know what it is about Ben Montague, but when I'm with him, I feel the constant need to kiss and fondle him, not to mention the frequent need to get him naked. But I like him for more than his scorching bod and his sexy smile. He's sweet and fun and smart too.

"How was your shopping trip?" I ask my parents as they shut the door.

"We checked off our entire Christmas to-do list," Mom says. "Got presents for you and Ben as well as Cameron, Amy, and the girls."

Ben looks a bit confused, so I explain, "Cameron is my brother. Amy is his wife, and they have two daughters."

"Ah. Thank you for the clarification."

I can't help it. I pinch his cheek and say to my parents, "Isn't Ben just the cutest? With his big vocabulary and British politeness."

"Oh, absolutely," Mom says. "He is the cutest."

Dad rolls his eyes. "Ignore them, Ben. Women like to say dumb things about us guys."

"I don't mind being called cute," Ben replies. "My friend Nick Hunter says it means a woman wants to sh—go out on a date with you."

I think he'd been about to say it means a woman wants to shag a man, but he caught himself before he blurted that out. Ben probably feels a little weird about chatting with my parents thirty seconds after we had mind-blowing sex in the hot tub.

As for me, I feel fabulous, not weird.

Mom and Dad set their bags down by the bar, and Ben and I follow them over there.

Dad sweeps his gaze over both of us. "Were you two out in the hot tub?"

"Yep. It's a beautiful day to be outside."

"I love it when the conditions are just right to make steam rise from the water."

"Sorry, no steam today."

Not from the water. But oh yeah, Ben and I made plenty of our own steam. Is saying "sorry" all the time a contagious disease? I just said it, but only once.

I survey all the bags my parents have brought home and finally realize an important fact. "You bought an awful lot of presents. Mailing all that stuff to Cameron and his brood will mean we need to buy a bunch of mailing boxes."

"No, we don't," Mom declares, as if I said a stupid thing. "They'll be here tomorrow to spend the holidays with us, here on the mountain."

"What? There's no room. Cam and Amy plus two kids?"

"Relax. We've got a plan."

They've got a plan? Mom and Dad already took the upstairs bedroom, and Ben has the sofa. What idea could my mom have dreamed up that would make more sleeping space magically appear?

I probably don't want to know. But she'll tell me anyway.

"Here's the plan," Mom says. "Your father and I will keep the upstairs room while you and Ben sleep in your bedroom."

"You want me to sleep with Ben?"

Dad chuckles. "Did you think we assumed you're still a virgin? We know our daughter has sex." He rolls his gaze toward Ben. "And we know who she's doing it with."

Oh. Dear. God. I never needed to hear my father say the phrase "doing it" while glancing meaningfully at my... What is Ben to me, anyway? "Friend" seems inadequate. He isn't exactly my boyfriend either. Ben Montague is my, um, companion. No, that doesn't sound at all like a pathetic attempt to downplay the fact we're having incredible sex.

But is that all we're doing?

"I don't think Sam is comfortable with that arrangement," Ben says. "I can sleep on the sofa bed like I've been doing."

"Afraid not, kid," Dad says. "Cam and Amy need the sofa bed. The girls are bringing sleeping bags, and they'll camp out on the floor. You'll just have to suck it up and share a room with Sam."

My father smirks at my, uh...boyfriend? My lover? *Ugh.* Neither one sounds right.

Ben looks at me, his brows raised.

I think he's asking a silent question. *Do you really want to share a bed with me?* The answer is yes, yes, yes—but not with my parents and my brother and his family sleeping in the same house with us. Not sure I can control my lust for Ben if we're both sleeping in my bed. Of course, he could sleep on the floor, but that would be so uncomfortable for him. He might get sore.

Sure, I'm worried about his physical well-being. That's why I get flutters in my tummy whenever I think about lying in the same bed with him all night, every night.

"Okay," I tell everyone. "Ben and I will share a bed."

Mom winks at me. "Good for you."

I have no idea what that means. My mother can't be congratulating me on scoring a hot Brit. Can she? A twenty-seven-year-old woman shouldn't get embarrassed when her mother implies she's happy her daughter is sleeping with a man she just met. But I do feel an eensy bit that way.

My brother and his brood will arrive tomorrow. Well, at least Ben's royal family isn't coming. Not sure I could handle meeting Princess Olivia. She sounds like a dragon lady, but Ben clearly loves his mom, so I guess she can't be that bad. Not sure how my family would react to a British invasion. Are his parents British? Ben said he has dual citizenship, but he didn't mention if his mom and dad have that too. Maybe they're only Mithorian or Mithori or whatever people from that island call themselves.

I'll ask Ben about that later. When we're cuddled up in bed together.

The four of us collaborate on dinner. Yes, four adults cram ourselves into the kitchen, which takes a bit of finagling, but we get the logistics worked out pretty quickly. It's fun to cook with my parents and Ben. We all tease each other and tell jokes. My mom reveals a few mildly embarrassing tidbits of info about me that I wish she hadn't told Ben, but he seems to love hearing all our family stories. Still, my sort-of boyfriend didn't need to hear about the time I tried to fix my ice skates with super glue and wound up gluing my hair to the skates instead.

That happened at a skating rink. With lots of people watching.

Ben seems to think the story is cute, and he shares a similarly embarrassing story from his youth too. I like him more every minute.

When it's time to go to sleep, Ben and I decide to start our bed-sharing tonight instead of waiting until tomorrow. Mom and Dad say good night to us and head upstairs. Then I lead Ben into my room—which is now our room, temporarily. The more time I spend with him, though, the more I want this to be our room for good.

Once we're snuggled under the covers, both lying on our sides facing each other, I have to ask the question that's been tormenting me. "Are you sure you want to stay for the Lockhart family invasion? I wouldn't blame you if you wanted to go to Hartmoor and spend the rest of your vacation in your friend's house."

"I don't want to leave. Unless you're having second thoughts about letting me stay."

"No doubts. I love having you here. But you don't need to feel obligated to hang around and meet the rest of my family. We can be a handful, especially as a horde."

"I doubt your brother and his lot are a horde. They're as lovely as you and your parents, I'm sure." He settles a hand on my arm, gliding it up and down slowly. "I want as much time with you as I can get. And it's nice to be around people who don't have rules for every sort of etiquette imaginable. My training in how to behave started so early that I can't remember when I wasn't being instructed in how to become a proper prince."

"That must be exhausting, always worrying about how you look and act."

"It can be. That's why I needed a break."

"Do you ever wish it could be more than a break from your life? I mean, you had a job in England. Maybe you could go back to that instead of becoming the crown prince again."

He sighs with so much resignation that I want to hug him. "I'm always the crown prince. It's my hereditary duty. Can't escape from it. The best I could hope for was a break from that world, but I always knew eventually I'd have to go home and leave behind the life I love."

"That's so sad. You should get the life you want, not the one you were born into and had no choice whether you wanted it or not."

He shuts his eyes and groans. "I'm whingeing, aren't I? Sorry. I want to enjoy this time with you and your family, not complain about all the things I can't have."

"Sure, I get that. But you aren't 'whingeing.' We're having a conversation." I brush my fingers through his hair, waiting until he opens his eyes before I say, "And you can have some of the things you want. Right now, you can get at least one of them."

"Which one would that be?"

I clasp his hand to my chest. "Take a wild guess."

"Ah, you mean to placate me with sex." His lips curve into a wicked smile. "Go on and do it."

My mouth decides now is the right time to gape open on a noisy yawn.

Ben kisses the tip of my nose. "You can placate me tomorrow. Let's go to sleep now."

"Okay. I am wiped out."

"Family can do that to you, in a good way."

I touch my lips to his. "You do that to me too, in the best way."

"Yes, I know. I'm brilliant at hot tub sex." He grins when I roll my eyes. "You make me feel so good that I never want to leave this bed."

I yawn again. "Me too."

He tugs the covers up to my shoulders. "Good night, Sam."

"Good night, Ben."

Every day since he came into my life, I feel like I never want this to end. How long do I need to know him before I can beg him to take me with him when he goes back to England? I'd go anywhere with Ben, even if that means visiting Mithoria and meeting the infamous Princess Olivia.

No, I can't be falling for Ben. It's crazy.

He slides an arm around me to pull my body snugly against his, with my head tucked under his chin. Wrapped up in Ben, I feel myself drifting off into the oblivion of sleep. But as I sink deeper and deeper into dreamland, one thought resurfaces.

Can I fall for a guy I've known for a matter of days?

Chapter Fifteen

Ben

The invasion has begun. After a quiet morning of lounging in the living room with Sam and her parents, watching the telly and playing card games, the proverbial ax has finally slammed down on my neck. I might have won three games of war, the card game, but now it's time for a different sort of battle. Sam's brother will arrive soon with his wife and two daughters. But it's not the females who worry me.

Worry? No, I am not concerned about how her brother will react to me. Absolutely not. I'm looking forward to meeting him. Looking forward while also chewing the inside of my cheek until I think I might have worn a hole through it. But no, that is not anxiety. It's, ah… Well, I'm excited to meet the rest of the Lockhart clan. That's all.

I do feel a touch nauseous, though. Must be the jalapeno chili Chuck made for lunch that's having that effect on me.

Yes, Sam's dad loves hot peppers. I've been warned that her brother Cameron loves them even more, so I should, as Chuck put it, "spray some polyurethane varnish on your tongue before you eat anything Cam cooked up." Brilliant. I can impress Sam's brother by hacking my guts out during dinner. I've never cared much for hot peppers, anyway.

But for Sam, I will eat them. Even if it kills me.

In the late afternoon, Sam's brother calls to let everyone know he and his family have just landed at the airport. They'll arrive in an hour or so. I do not get nauseous when I hear that news. It must've been the chili after all.

Though everyone tells me I don't need to "gussy up" for the arrival of the last few Lockharts, I decide to exchange my jeans and T-shirt for khaki trousers and a button-down shirt with the top button undone. This is dress casual or some such bollocks. I don't want to look like a posh prince, but I also don't want to seem like a slob either. I've never spent this much time worrying about my clothes.

When I walk out into the living room wearing my dress casual outfit, Chuck smirks. "Didn't we say you don't need to get all gussied up? It's just my kid and his kids. Amy and the girls don't care if you look like a CEO or a frat boy."

"I know, but I wanted to make a good first impression."

"Didn't worry about that when Judy and I got here." He waggles his eyebrows. "As I recall, you were buck naked."

"You surprised us. And I was half-naked, wearing my boxers."

"Oh yeah, that's a big difference."

"Sorry. I know I'm being a bit precious about this, but I wanted to make a better first impression this time."

"I get that. But you don't need to try so hard."

"Right." I glance down at my clothes. "Should I change into something less… I don't know."

"You're fine. Relax, kid. It'll be over soon."

I might feel more relaxed if he hadn't said it will be over soon. That sounds awfully final. What will be over? I'm not walking away from Sam, no matter what her brother says or does. Even if she tells me to leave, I will do whatever it takes to convince her to let me stay.

Sam is in the kitchen with her mother right now. They seem to be discussing something important, speaking softly and leaning in close to each other. I assume they didn't hear anything Chuck just told me, and I can't help wondering what sort of conversation they're having that requires whispering.

Chuck peeks out the window that overlooks the front porch. Then he throws his head back and shouts, "I see a car. They're almost here."

Judy and Sam emerge from the kitchen to join us near the front door.

I do not feel nauseous. Not even a little.

Sam sidles up to me, slipping her hand into mine. She raises onto her tiptoes to whisper, "Stop tensing up. Cameron is a nice guy, not an assassin."

Was I tensing up? Since my shoulders have started to ache just a little, I think I must have been doing that. Pulling in a deep breath, I exhale it slowly and let the tension sift away. I suspect it's Sam, not my deep breathing, that relaxes me. She smells good, though not like perfume. It's just her natural, indescribable scent.

A knock rattles the front door.

Chuck swings it open and grins. "Merry Christmas! Come on in, guys. We've got a little surprise for you."

A tall man with broad shoulders and a dark beard that matches his dark hair saunters into the house. A petite redhead follows him, and two girls trail after her. One has auburn hair while the other has dark hair, like her father. The girls don't look old enough or tall enough to be teenagers, but they aren't small children either.

Cameron Lockhart gives his parents quick hugs, then approaches me and Sam. "Who's this guy? I'm guessing he's the surprise Dad mentioned."

"Um, yeah," Sam says, hunching her shoulders. "I guess he is the surprise."

I thrust my hand out to Sam's brother. "Bennett Montague. But you can call me Ben."

"Cameron Lockhart," he says a bit cautiously as he shakes my hand. "Where are you from? Don't sound American."

"I—Well, it's a long story. Essentially, I'm British."

"Uh-huh. Essentially? You must know where you're from. So why are you being cagey about it?"

I don't think I'm doing that. Am I? Well, maybe a little. I'd hoped to delay the "I'm a crown prince" rubbish until later, but clearly, Cameron wants answers now. I am sleeping with his sister, so I can't blame him for that.

"I'd be happy to explain," I say. "But it's a long story, so you might want to get settled in first."

"Okay. I'll let you wriggle out of it for now."

"Thank you, Cameron."

"Everybody calls me Cam. Guess you might as well too."

I've only just realized something about their names, and I have to speak up. "You're Cam and Sam? I have mates called Rick and Nick, who are brothers, but they're twins."

"Sam and I aren't twins. Our parents liked the rhyming first syllables in our names, that's all. I'm five years older than my sister." Cameron squints at me the way Chuck likes to do. "Not sure I like my sister shacking up with a foreigner who's cagey about where he comes from."

"It's none of your business," Sam says. She makes a shooing motion with her hands. "Stop harassing Ben and go get settled in, like he said."

Cameron glances around the room. "Uh, I am settled. We're sleeping in here, right? That's what Mom and Dad said."

"Oh, right. I forgot."

Maybe she's a little anxious too.

Not that I am or ever was anxious. Bloody hell. Of course I was.

Sam grabs my arm and drags me toward the hallway. "We'll be back in a minute. Go ahead and find someplace to put your stuff. Anywhere is good."

Either she's desperate for a shag, or she wants to give me instructions on how to behave around her family. It's probably the latter. I have no illusions I'm so good in bed that she can't go a few hours without sex. It's been more like days without sex, though. Hard to find a private moment with her parents on the premises, and now her brother and his family are here too. We may never shag again. But oddly, that doesn't bother me. I like spending time with Sam even if we don't do anything other than talk.

Once we're inside the bedroom with the door closed, she releases my arm. "How are you doing with all this Lockhart family craziness?"

"Fine. What about you?"

"They're my family. I've dealt with them all my life, so I'm used to it." She studies me while biting her lip. "Are you sure you're okay with this?"

"Your family? Yes. If I can handle a parade of greedy aristocratic girls, I can handle you lot." I lean against the wall beside the door. "Did you drag me in here just to make sure I'm coping with your family?"

"Not entirely. I needed a bit of a break too."

"Maybe we could go out on a date sometime, in the evening like a proper couple. That would be a nice break, wouldn't you say?"

Her lips curve into a sweet smile that swiftly becomes a grin. "That sounds perfect. You're a genius, Ben."

"Thank you," I say with a laugh. "But I'm not that amazing. Hold off on the 'genius' bit until after you see what I plan for our big date."

"Ooh, a *big* date. I like the sound of that."

Maybe I should've considered the ramifications before I announced I want to take her on a "big" date like a "proper" couple. She might be expecting something lavish, but I have no ruddy idea how to impress a girl on a date. I've never been that good at crafting romantic gestures. For Sam, I will make the effort and hopefully come up with something she'll love. She did rescue me from a snowy death, so I owe her a special night out.

Now, I just have to plan the event. No problem. I might be getting slightly nauseous again, but that will pass.

Sam takes my face in her hands and kisses me. "You're wonderful, Ben. I've never met a man like you before. You know, the kind who doesn't treat women like blow-up sex dolls or a free maid service."

"What sort of arseholes have you dated?"

"Every sort there is."

"No wonder you moved out here to the back of beyond." I pull her into my arms and brush my lips across hers. "I would never treat any woman that way, not even the ones who treat me like their ticket to the high life."

"Guess we've both had a bad time with dating."

"Not anymore. Getting stranded in a blizzard was the best thing that ever happened to me."

She nuzzles my cheek. "You're so sweet. I'm looking forward to our date. But right now, we need to go out there and act like grown-ups instead of hiding in my room."

"You're right. Let's go."

Hand in hand, we head back out into the living room where the rest of the Lockharts are laughing and generally having a good time. I can't remember the last time I had fun with my parents and my sister. I love them, but we aren't exactly the good-time kind of family. I remember when we were, but that was before my grandfather died and my dad became Prince Leighton of Mithoria.

Maybe we've all gotten uptight. Maybe we can change that.

Not today, though.

Cameron and Amy's two daughters, Ella and Lily, turn out to be sweet, clever girls who make everyone laugh with their jokes and magic tricks. Yes, a ten-year-old and an eight-year-old have both mastered magic. They pull a plush rabbit toy out of a hat and do card tricks too. When Ella tries to teach me how to make a card disappear, I cock it up, naturally.

"I've been doing this for three years," she informs me. "I practiced a lot."

Yes, I need a ten-year-old to soothe my wounded ego. I don't feel too bad, though, since Cameron can't pull off any of his daughter's tricks either. He sends the card flying halfway across the room when he tries to make the thing disappear. At least I only dropped the card on my lap. Maybe I shouldn't feel smug about not doing as badly at children's card tricks as Cameron did, but I can't help it. He keeps making sly comments about me and Sam sharing a bedroom, so I feel justified in my smugness about not bollocksing up card tricks as badly as Sam's brother did.

Now if I can manage not to screw up my big date with Sam…

Chapter Sixteen

We spend the next few days with my family, all six of them, and don't have much time to think about our big date. At least, I don't have the extra space in my brain to think about it. As it turns out, Ben spends a lot of time secretly plotting how to make our first official night out a special one. I wouldn't have minded if we just went to a restaurant for dinner. But no, the crown prince decides to go all out.

No man has ever done that for me.

Exactly one week after the night I found Ben on the road, snowbound in his dead car, we have our date. Ben went to town yesterday with my dad and Cameron so they could do secret "man-shopping" for Christmas. Yeah, Chuck Lockhart actually spoke those words. Luckily, "man-shopping" didn't involve bringing strange guys home with them. They bought gifts for us ladies, but we won't know what they're giving us until Christmas, which is one week away. All Ben would tell me was that he "splashed out," which he explained is British for going hog wild. That's my translation. He actually said, "It means you spend a lot of money without giving a toss how much the things you buy cost."

"I thought you technically weren't rich because your mother cut you off as punishment for staying in England."

"That's true. I may not have shedloads of money, but I've saved up enough from my job at the spa to spoil you this Christmas."

No guy has ever wanted to spoil me before. So I think I'll let him do that.

He did tell me about one thing he bought during the man-shopping spree, and I'm about to see it—as soon as I change into the outfit I've picked out for our big date. Ben bought a suit for this occasion, but I'm wearing a dress I already own instead of something new. If I'd known about his plans, I would've gone shopping for a new dress. When I told Ben that this afternoon when he shared his clothing news, he kissed me and told me he doesn't care if I wear a burlap sack because I'm the sexiest, most beautiful woman in the world.

I know he's not just sucking up. He means it.

Since this is a special night, I shaved my legs and colored my hair. Yeah, blonde is not my natural color. So what? A girl can change her hair if she wants. Maybe I'll go red in a few months if I feel like it. I bet Ben would love that. If I dyed my hair purple, he'd probably love that too. He's the sweetest, sexiest, most amazing man I've ever met.

Dressed in my favorite outfit—a cobalt-blue halter dress with matching high heels and a matching clutch—I swing the bedroom door open and step into the hall.

Ben stands in front of the bathroom door directly across the hall, as if he's been waiting for me.

Holy shit. He looks so damn good that I want to drag him into our room and screw him all night long. To hell with dinner. I want him.

Ben is wearing a charcoal suit with a matching tie and a white dress shirt. He's done something to his hair, like he slicked it back but not so much that it looks like lacquer. No, he looks like a movie star. When he walks up to me and holds out his hand, I get a fluttery sensation in my tummy. "May I have the honor of escorting you to the finest restaurant in New Hampshire?"

I slip my hand into his. "Yes, you may. Damn, you're one hot Brit. The hottest man on earth, actually, with or without the accent."

"Thank you, love." He lifts our hands to kiss mine. "You are stunning. I love that frock, but it's your body that makes the dress."

"Wow. I've never received a compliment like that one before."

"You deserve to be showered with compliments and gifts. You deserve everything, Samantha."

"Thank you, Bennett. You are an incredible man."

I love it when he says my full name. I love every word he speaks, actually, but most of all the way my name sounds coming from his lips.

He guides me out into the living room where my entire family is watching a movie on TV. They pause their show when they see us, and every head turns to stare at us.

"Hey look, it's James Bond and Miss Moneypenny," Cameron says with a sly grin. "Are you off to break into Fort Knox and stop the bad guy from stealing all the loot?"

Amy pokes her husband in the side. "He means you two look fantastic and we hope you have a wonderful evening. Isn't that right, Cam?"

"Sure. Isn't that what I said?"

"Miss Moneypenny didn't go on missions with James Bond, anyway. Get your movie references right, honey."

Cam winks at me. "Have fun, sis."

"Yeah, have a great time," Dad says. "You deserve it."

My brother squints at Ben. "Don't get my sister into any trouble."

"I wouldn't dream of it."

Ben threads his fingers through mine as we put on our coats and leave the house. We get into my car, but Ben insists on driving so our destination will be a surprise. He opens my door for me and holds my hand as I get inside, the way gentlemen do in old movies. I didn't think anyone did that these days. But Bennett Montague isn't like anyone else. He's one of a kind, and I love that about him.

Maybe his mother taught him to be chivalrous. She is a princess after all, and he is the crown prince.

I'm going on a date with a member of a royal family. Wow.

As we drive through the deepening twilight, I start to get an inkling of where we're going. The road signs give me clues. We've turned onto the highway Ben should've taken when he got lost one week ago tonight.

"We're going to Hartmoor?" I say. "Didn't know there were any fancy restaurants there."

"Did you want a posh restaurant? I thought you'd prefer the sort where they give you a bib and a trough of lobster, with a nutcracker to break open the shells and a vat of melted butter to dip the meat in."

"Ha-ha. We wouldn't be dressed like royalty if you were taking me to a place like that."

"Fair point." He glances at me sideways. "Yes, we are going to Hartmoor. But there's a new restaurant in the village. My mate Chance Dixon told me about it. He lives in Hartmoor, and he was a major investor in that new restaurant, which opened six months ago. It's the first high-end eatery in the area."

"That sounds amazing."

"I talked to Chance a few days ago, and he swears The Hartmoor Inn is very posh but not so upscale that you'll feel like you shouldn't belch while you're in the restaurant."

"Belch? A lady never does that."

"You did that the other night. After your brother fed us five-alarm chili with jalapeno cheese bread."

I can't help smiling when I remember that meal. "Your face turned red when you ate a big mouthful of it."

"Felt like my head was about to explode. Can't understand how anyone could eat like that."

"I think Cam has a secret mouth spray that protects his taste buds."

"That would explain it. Does Cameron eat that way all the time?"

"No. Amy doesn't like super-hot stuff. He was testing you."

"Testing me how? To see if I have a strong digestive system?"

I can't help laughing. "He wanted to make sure you're not a wuss. Cameron thinks I need to be protected."

"Didn't you tell him how you rescued me? I was minutes away from becoming a human icicle."

"He knows about that. But Cam still treats me like I'm a little girl. Most of the time, I think it's sweet." I gaze out at the snowy landscape whizzing past my window. "Once in a while, it can be annoying. But he acts that way because he cares."

"You have a wonderful family. I wish I could stay here with all of you forever."

"What about your job in Cockshire?"

"Oh, yes. Forgot about that for a minute."

Maybe I want him to stay here forever too. I could go with him back to England. My job is done over the internet, so I could live anywhere. Ben hasn't asked me to go with him. He suggested he might want to stay here.

We enter the village of Hartmoor just as the last ribbons of sunset sink below the horizon. I've never been to this town, so I can't resist gawking at the historic buildings and the quaint houses as we wend our way down the streets. Finally, we pull into a small parking lot in front of what looks like an old two-story house that's been converted into a restaurant. Ben parks near the building.

When I reach for the handle on my door, Ben declares, "Do not move, Sam."

I've never heard him sound so commanding before. And yeah, it makes me hot for him.

He comes around to my side and opens the door, offering me his hand. "Now you may disembark, my lady."

"You're the royal. I'm just an average American."

"Not for tonight. You are my queen, and I have a splendid feast arranged for you."

As I get out of the car, I glance around. "Why aren't there any other vehicles here?"

"Because I arranged for us to have a private meal."

"Really? I've never had a restaurant all to myself."

"Mind sharing it with me?" he asks with a smirk.

"I meant all to myself with you."

"Ah, I see." He holds out his bent arm and waits for me to hook mine around it. "Allow me to escort you into our banquet hall."

"You're committed to the royal-speak tonight, aren't you? Don't get me wrong, I like it." I snuggle up to him with my cheek on his upper arm. "But you don't need to impress me. You've already done that plenty."

"Have I? Not sure how I did it."

"By being you. I liked you a lot before you told me you're a crown prince."

He pauses with his free hand on the doorknob. "You liked me when I was just Ben the massage therapist?"

"Yes. Did you think I was faking it before I found out you're royalty? I had sex with you before that."

Ben scratches the back of his neck, his head bowed. "I know you aren't the sort who lusts after a title, but I guess I can't believe a woman like you wants me for more than sex."

"Then what's the deal with this big date? You obviously want more with me. I want more with you, for sure."

"More what?"

"Everything." I lay a hand on his cheek. "We've known each other for a week, and already I don't want you to leave. You're important to me."

"I feel the same way. But..." He shuts his eyes and sighs, then looks at me again. "I don't know if our lives can ever mesh."

Yeah, I'm not sure about that either. I mean, Ben the massage therapist is just a regular guy. But then there's Bennett Worthington Montague, crown prince of Mithoria. It's a little scary to think about that part of his life because I don't know if I could handle the pressure.

"Just for tonight," I say, "let's forget about everything and enjoy our date."

"All right. I can do that."

He leads me through the door and into a short hallway that has muted lighting and ends at the main restaurant area where I can see tables with chairs, and booths tucked into secluded corners. The lighting is just as subdued in that area as it is here in the entryway. Soft, romantic music plays, but I don't think that's a recording. It sounds like a jazz ensemble playing an easygoing, sensual tune.

"Since we have the restaurant all to ourselves," Ben tells me, "I've arranged for live music to make sure we have the perfect atmosphere. Turns out there's a jazz trio based in Hartmoor, so I hired them."

"The music sounds fabulous. This whole night is fabulous."

A waiter approaches, greeting us with a smile and guiding us into the main area of the restaurant. Since we have the whole place to ourselves, we choose a booth near where the jazz trio is set up, but not so close that we have no privacy. We only just got here and already I want to unzip Ben's pants and ride him until we both scream. It's the suit doing that to me. He genuinely does look like a sophisticated spy. If he wants to torture secrets out of me, I won't mind at all.

Ben takes my hand as I slide onto the curved bench seat, then he slides in beside me.

Our date has officially begun.

Chapter Seventeen

I love my life. Never have I said that before, not even when I was living in Cockshire and doing my job, which I love. I always had an enormous boulder hanging over my head, held up by only the slenderest rope, and I knew one day that monstrosity would crash down on me. Yes, I'm comparing my life as a crown prince to being squashed by a boulder. Why not? Every time I go back to Mithoria, I feel like I'm being compressed by the intense pressure of everyone else's expectations, not to mention all those greedy girls.

Now I'm with Sam. We're on a date. So yeah, I love my life right now.

While we peruse the food offerings, Sam leans into me so we can both look at the same menu. She points to items and oohs at them like she hasn't seen lobster or filet mignon before. I'm sure she has, but Sam always gets enthusiastic about…everything. I love that about her. Even shopping for a snowsuit is fun as long as I'm with her.

Now, shopping with her father and brother is another story. I enjoyed my outing with "the boys," as Judy called us, but I can never tell for sure if they like me or if they're sizing me up and debating whether to toss me out of the car on the way home. I'm joking, of course. They like me. I like them too, and I think Cameron has finally decided I'm not a "slick foreigner trying to make time with Sam." Yes, Cam said that. Well, what he actually said was "you better not just be some slick foreigner trying to make time with my baby sister so you can get another notch in your belt."

I rarely wear a belt, so he has nothing to worry about.

After we order our food, I get up and offer my hand to Sam. "May I have this dance?"

She smiles and shimmies across the bench to take my hand, letting me help her up. "I'd love to dance with you anytime, anywhere."

I lead her out onto the little dance floor, right in front of the musicians, who are playing a sensual melody with jazz styling. I've never been a big fan of jazz, but the restaurant owner had recommended this group, and I thought Sam might enjoy the music. But now I find I'm enjoying it too. With Sam in my arms as we glide across the floor, I feel better than I have in years, happy and relaxed and free of all the weight that's been pressing down on me for so long. She feels right in my arms, like I was always meant to find this woman and dance with her in this place.

That's sentimental rubbish, I know. But I refuse to worry about that tonight.

She rests her cheek on my chest, her arms twined behind my neck, and the sweetest little smile curls her lips. I link my hands at the small of her back, and our dancing becomes foot shuffling as we let the music lull us into a near trance. I'm entranced for sure, by the beautiful, amazing woman who has her warm body molded to mine.

The song ends. As another melody starts up in its place, I take Sam back to the booth. The waiter is just bringing our food, so we admire the offerings while they're laid out before us on the table. Everything smells incredible. Maybe this is the best restaurant in New Hampshire after all, or maybe I would love any food, even a block of smelly cheese, simply because I'm with Sam. She makes me feel like a normal bloke who's on a normal date with the most wonderful girl on earth. But I know, sooner or later, I'll have to face up to my problems—and my duties.

Not tonight, though.

Sam and I chat to each other while we eat, sharing funny stories about our family and friends. Yes, I do actually have humorous stories to tell about my royal family. When I relate an incident that involves my mother and a salivating poodle, Sam laughs so hard her eyes water. I love making her laugh and making her smile, but I especially love making her come. I wish we could do that tonight, but with her whole family in residence at the little cabin, I don't see how we can shag without keeping everyone awake and frightening the children too.

Once Sam is done laughing about the poodle incident, she lays a hand on my thigh and kisses my cheek.

"What was that for?" I ask.

"I love hearing your stories. You haven't wanted to talk about your family much, or at least it seemed that way to me."

"Maybe I don't say much about them, but it's not on purpose." I try very hard not to squirm when she skates her hand up and down my thigh. "It's just that thinking about my family reminds me of all the rubbish I'll have to deal with when I finally go home."

"And by 'go home,' you mean go back to Mithoria."

"Yes. I've been avoiding it, but I can't do that forever."

She chews on her lip for a moment, watching me with an expression I can't figure out. "I get why your mother is determined to find you a wife. But a mom should want what's best for her son, not force him to do something that will make him miserable."

"I know I've probably made Mum sound like a dictator, but she isn't like that. Not most of the time." I do squirm now, though not because Sam is touching me. "I knew from the start my time in England would be finite. I also knew running away to New Hampshire wouldn't spare me for long either."

"But you're happy in England and here with me."

I've never been happier in my entire life than I am tonight with her. Should I tell her that? Not sure there's any point to admitting it. Like I just told her, my time here is finite. Maybe I shouldn't have gotten involved with her. Maybe I'm a selfish bastard.

"What are you worrying about now?" she asks, her voice tender, not annoyed.

"Everything." I slump forward, my elbows on the table, and cradle my forehead in my palms. "I'm sorry, Sam. I've been selfish, and I've led you to believe we could have a real relationship. But I don't get what I want. My duty is to Mithoria. I need to go home and resign myself to what I've always known I'd need to do, eventually."

"You're leaving? But it's not even Christmas yet."

"If I stay, it will just make it harder when I finally go."

Her fingers crook into my thigh. "But I'm not ready to say goodbye. Please, Ben, stay through Christmas."

I don't want to leave her yet either, but I should do it. Shouldn't I? Knowing what the right thing is has gotten so much harder since I met her.

"Sorry," I say, sitting up straight. "I'm ruining our date, aren't I? Let's forget about all that for now and have a good time, like we were doing before I decided to whinge about my life."

"I've been assuming 'whinge' means to complain."

"Yes. And I've been doing too much of that."

She squeezes my thigh. "No, you haven't. But I agree we should focus on enjoying the holidays and let the rest work itself out." She holds out her hand like she wants to shake mine. "Deal?"

I slip my palm into hers. "Deal."

We finish our meal, telling each other more stories, and we keep talking while we enjoy dessert. Every time I look at Sam in that dress, I want to make love to her. Not just shag her, though I love doing that too. I want to make love to her in the truest sense of the term and show her how much she means to me. Because, while I've been watching her reactions to my stories, and the way her face lights up when she talks about her family, I realized something vital.

I'm falling in love with her.

But it's much too soon to tell her that. I think. Do women want men to declare their feelings the instant they realize the truth? Not sure. I've never been adept at puzzling out what women want. With Sam, though, it's different. She's different. I want to share my realization with her, but I can't help worrying she might think I'm insane. We met a week ago, after all.

So, I think I'll wait to tell her.

After dessert, we take one more spin around the dance floor before we head back to the cabin that's become a boarding house for wayward Lockharts. I love them all, but the house does seem rather crowded these days. And yes, I desperately want to get a leg over with Sam, but we both agree it's not the right time. I don't share my revelation with her, so she has no idea I want to get her naked so I can express my feelings for her in the only way I know how to do that without cocking it up. The last time I tried to tell a girl how much I liked her, I wound up spilling a plate of spaghetti and meatballs all over her lap.

Maybe I haven't always been suave with the ladies, like Nick Hunter or Reese Dixon, but I've done well enough. I've never tried to tell a woman I'm falling for her, though, and I think that's why I can't talk myself into doing that.

We crawl into bed together and fall asleep quickly, exhausted in the best way from our big night out as an official couple. I love sleeping with Sam, holding her in my arms while we both drift off, and especially the bit where I wake up in the morning to find her body sprawled half on top of me and her hair tickling my chin. I just lie here for a long time—half an hour, according to the old-fashioned alarm clock on the nightstand—because I can't bear to disturb her when she's sleeping. I love the little smile on her lips. It makes me wonder what she's dreaming about, but I won't wake her even to find out the answer.

When she finally rouses, she rolls onto her back and stretches her entire body, while a loud yawn splits her mouth open. She flips onto her side again to drape an arm across my chest. "Morning, Ben."

"Good morning, Sam. Sleep well?"

"Mm-hm." She glides her hand across my chest, swirling her fingers around my nipple. "Maybe we could have stealth sex. I'm feeling so deprived."

"Stealth sex? Am I meant to become invisible?"

"No. Just quiet."

I palm her arse. "You're the one who screams my name."

"There's also the issue of the bed creaking. Maybe if we do it in the shower…"

A laugh bursts out of me. "The shower? The bathroom door has no lock, and the last time I took a shower, your brother waltzed into the room and started brushing his teeth."

"The shower stall is frosted glass. He couldn't see anything."

"Still, I think we should hold off on any kind of sex until we have more privacy." I give her arse a squeeze. "Can't control myself when I'm with you."

"Okay, we'll wait."

Not too long, though. I need to feel her body wrapped around my cock soon, or I'll go insane.

I kiss the tip of her nose. "Why don't you have a shower while I go out there and try to talk Cameron out of making scrambled eggs with cayenne pepper in them and hot sauce on top."

She laughs as she hops off the bed. "Better get used to the spicy stuff if you want to join this family."

"I can handle all the spicy stuff. You know that."

And yes, we both know I wasn't talking about food.

Sam throws on a robe and grabs some clothes, then sashays across the hall to the bathroom. I get dressed and venture into the living room where the other Lockharts have already gathered. Ella and Lily are playing a board game I don't recognize, and they seem to be having a jolly good time considering how much they giggle. Cam and Amy have taken over the kitchen, and I think they're making some sort of egg dish. I'm hardly a foodie, so I can't figure out exactly what they've got in that frying pan.

Chuck and Judy sit on stools on this side of the island, watching their son and his wife whip up breakfast.

I perch on the stool beside Chuck's. "Good morning. What's for breakfast?"

"Frittatas," Chuck says. "That's our best guess, anyway. Cam isn't exactly a gourmet chef, and Amy seems to have her doubts about whatever that is in the pan."

Cameron glances over his shoulder at his father and puckers his lips. "It *is* frittatas, Dad. And who said Amy has her doubts? She loves my cooking just as much as I love hers."

"That's your story, hey?"

"It's a fact." Cam waves a spatula toward his wife. "Tell them, Amy. I rock the frittatas."

Their discussion keeps going, but I'm not actively listening anymore. I like to just watch these people, the way they interact with each other, their teasing sarcasm, the way they act as if I've always been a member of their family. Not that I am now. But they treat me like I am.

Sam ambles out of the hallway, now fully dressed, and stops at my stool. She wraps an arm around my waist, leaning into me. When she smiles at me, I smile right back. I might actually be grinning like an idiot, but I don't care. Warmth spreads through me, and I can't stop looking at her. When she kisses my cheek, I get an odd fluttery sensation in my chest.

Oh yes. I am definitely in love with Samantha Lockhart.

Chapter Eighteen

We spend the entire morning with my family, though honestly, it feels like Ben has become a part of our family despite the fact my parents and my brother met Ben less than a week ago. They love him, I can tell. Cam shows his affection by mercilessly teasing Ben, but my boyfriend can handle it. He teases Cam right back. Dad expresses his fondness by smacking Ben on the back so hard that the poor guy stumbles. Dad only does that once in a while, and I think my guy is getting used to it.

I wonder what Ben's family would think of me.

Just before lunch, we all go outside to play in the snow. Cam and Dad insist that kind of thing is strictly for children and "silly grown women." Well, I am proud to be a silly grown woman. I know when to be serious, but I pride myself on my ability to enjoy any activity with gusto. When I'd first met Ben, he hadn't seemed like the gusto type, but I'd been wrong about that. Maybe he's different here with me in New Hampshire, but I doubt that. He's a massage therapist. That doesn't sound like a job for an uptight guy.

Ben is definitely not uptight.

We find a nice, big open area behind the house that has a good slope for sledding, then we get out the sleds and have fun. Luckily, my grandfather loved this kind of activity, so he left several types of sleds in the shed behind the house. Ella and Lily take the disk-shaped models while Cam commandeers the traditional wooden one. That leaves an inflatable sled for me and Ben to share. My parents opt for watching the rest of us from the comfort of lawn chairs, and they seem to be having a great time, laughing and cheering us on.

I love sledding with Ben. Because it's fun, yes. But I also love having him behind me, his body cradling mine while we zip down the slope. We pass by Ella and Lily, Cam too, and reach the bottom first. But we're having so much fun that we don't slow ourselves down fast enough, and we tip over into the snow. Still, that makes us laugh. No one has ever made me laugh as much as Ben does.

He winds up on top of me because I somehow got flipped over when we fell off the sled. Not that I mind being pinned down by Ben's hot body. The inflatable sled lies on top of us, the perfect cover for making out so no one can see that's what we're doing.

When Cam plucks the sled off us, he catches me and Ben in the act. We're kissing, not having sex. But my brother pretends to be horrified, making a ridiculously exaggerated face. "You nearly killed my sister with your bad sledding skills, and now you're molesting her in front of everyone. I should rip you a new one, pal."

Cam's squinty glare is so phony that nobody could mistake it for an actual threat. He waggles his eyebrows too, which makes it crystal clear he's teasing my boyfriend.

Ben picks me up and sets me down on my feet, then he brushes snow off my hat and coat. "You're a beautiful snow angel."

Cameron pretends to gag. "Don't make me hurl."

"How about a sled race?" Ben asks. "Just you and me."

"You're on. Be prepared to lose, Romeo."

"Oh, you're the one who will be flat on his arse in the snow watching me cross the finish line."

Male bonding is a bizarre ritual.

Just then, Lily and Ella finally reach the bottom of the hill. They were too busy doing the sledding version of wheelies to care if they got to the bottom first. When they hear about Ben and Cam's sled duel, the girls shriek and start betting on who will win. I would've thought they'd both root for their father, but Ella decides to defect to Ben's team. Cam clutches his chest and pretends he's having a heart attack when his daughter makes her choice.

Ella giggles.

Yeah, my brother is weird. Okay, my whole family is weird. Guess that includes me too.

We trudge back up the hill to the starting point for what Cam announces is the Great Brit versus American Sledding Apocalypse. What does the end of the world have to do with a silly sled race? Cameron is definitely the weirdest Lockhart. Both men take disk sleds to make sure the playing field is even. If one of them had the inflatable sled, it might skew the race or something. But I stop listening to Cam, Ben, and my dad discussing the details of the race. I'm distracted by staring at Ben.

He's so…wonderful. I've known him for such a short time, but I feel like I've known him all my life. That's dumb, I know. It's how I feel, though. Ever since Bennett Montague crashed into my life, I've been happier than ever before, and that's all thanks to the crown prince. Even before I knew about his background and his title, Ben had already impressed me with his sweetness, his humor, his sexiness, and so many other amazing qualities. I don't want him to go back to England or Mithoria. I want him to stay here with me forever, in this cozy cabin, sharing a bed and sharing our lives.

I freeze, not even blinking, my gaze still locked on Ben. I think I've just had an epiphany. And the longer I gaze at Ben, the stronger this sensation inside me gets. It feels warm and soft and yet strong too, like a weight has pressed down on my chest, but not in a bad way. No, I like this feeling. Even as that weight settles on my chest, I experience a sensation of weightlessness like my entire body is floating above the ground.

Oh yeah, I've had an epiphany all right. I'm in love with Ben. *Holy shit.*

Ben and Cam get on their sleds and make engine revving noises as if their sleds are race cars. Dad and I stand behind the competitors with our hands on their backs, ready to send them careening down the slope. I'm behind Ben, while Dad is behind Cam. Ella and Lily count down to liftoff. And no, I don't care that I'm mixing metaphors. This is exactly like NASCAR meets NASA because I have a feeling these two men will want to rocket down the hill.

"Ten, nine, eight," the girls holler. "Seven, six, five—"

Dad winks at me and smirks.

I have no idea why he did that.

"Four, three, two, one," the girls shout. "Go!"

Dad and I give our guys a strong shove, and they're off.

Ben and Cam rush down the slope, shouting things I can't make out. From their tone of voice, though, I'm pretty sure they're razzing each other. I clasp my hands, bouncing on my toes and biting down on my lip. Should I be rooting for my brother? I don't know what sled-race etiquette would say, but I can't do anything except hope Ben beats Cam.

The race is a dead heat.

"Go, Ben, go!" I holler.

Lily and Amy shout their support for Cameron, but Ella stands beside me, yelling for Ben. Mom and Dad don't declare their preference, though they do whistle and clap.

Cam inches ahead of Ben, but he makes the mistake of gloating by pumping his fist in the air. That makes his sled veer sideways, slowing him down just enough that Ben zips past him and crosses the finish line first.

We don't have an actual finish line, though. It's imaginary.

Ben reaches the bottom of the hill well ahead of Cameron and wins the race.

I jump up and down, waving my hands in the air, and scream, "Woo-hoo! Go, Ben! You rock!"

Maybe that's a dumb thing to scream, but I don't care. My guy won, and I'm so happy about that.

The guys shake hands, then begin their slog back up the hill.

As soon as they reach us, I throw my arms around Ben. "Congratulations, you won. I'm so proud of you."

"Proud?" he says with a laugh. "It was a bloody silly race. I didn't win the Nobel Prize."

"No, but you do get a prize for winning. Maybe it's not a Nobel, but I think you'll like it."

I wrap my arms around his neck and hoist myself onto my toes so I can plaster my mouth to his.

"Ew," Ella and Lily say.

When I peel my lips away from Ben's, he glances around like he's a little embarrassed by my public display of affection. But he recovers from the shock swiftly and slings his arms around me to pull me in for a kiss that's much more passionate than the one I just gave him.

The girls giggle this time.

Cam whistles.

By the time Ben releases me, I'm breathless and my cheeks feel hot. The rest of me feels hot too, but in a different way that's highly inappropriate considering that my family is watching us. I don't care, though. I love Ben, and I need to tell him that so badly. Keeping secrets has never been my strong suit.

"Who wants hot cocoa?" Mom asks.

Ella and Lily shout, "Me! Me!"

Cam jumps and down while making a ridiculous fake-excited face. "Ooh! Ooh! Me too!"

The girls laugh.

Okay, the adults laugh too. My brother is so weird, but we all love him anyway.

"Why don't you guys go inside and get the cocoa started," I say. "Ben and I want to stay out here for a minute."

Cameron waggles his eyebrows. "Somebody wants to smooch in private."

Amy grabs her husband's arm and drags him toward the house. Lily and Ella trail after them, giggling the whole time, and my parents bring up the rear.

Once everyone has gone inside, I face Ben. "There's something I need to tell you."

"A sentence like that rarely means good news."

"Well, I guess whether it's good or bad depends on how you feel about it."

He clasps my hands. "You can tell me anything, Sam."

Just do it, I command myself. Then I swallow hard because a lump of iron seems to have gotten lodged in my throat. "I love you, Ben."

"I love you too, Sam."

"Really?"

He grins. "Yes, really. I realized this morning that I'm in love with you. We haven't known each other long, so I was afraid to tell you how I feel. Thought you might think I'm barmy."

"If you are, then I am too. And it feels wonderful."

We're both grinning now, like brainless idiots. Who cares? I finally found a nice guy who makes me feel good in every way imaginable. We suit each other so well that it seems impossible and probably insane, considering we met a week ago. But I refuse to overanalyze this. Ben is amazing. He makes me feel things I never imagined I could feel, and I love him. Nothing else matters.

"It does feel bloody wonderful," he says, tugging me closer. "Maybe it was fate that brought us together, or maybe it was dumb luck. I don't care. All I know is I love being with you. I love *you*, full stop."

He drags me into his arms for a scorching kiss, one that melts every muscle in my body and leaves me sagging against him. Ben always does this to me.

When I regain the ability to speak, I say, "I need you to make love to me tonight, Ben. Screw what anybody else might hear."

"I'd love to do that." He brushes stray hairs away from my eyes. "But I think we'd better go inside now and drink cocoa."

"Yep, we should."

Hand in hand, we wander back into the house, and we keep flashing each other shy smiles like we're teenage virgins about to have sex for the first time. We sit on stools at the bar to drink our cocoa, and I think everyone can tell something has changed between me and Ben. Nobody says anything about it, though. My family might be strange and goofy, but they've got tact.

Just as we're all finishing off our cocoa, the doorbell rings.

I jump off my stool. "I'll see who that is."

"Don't be long," Ben whispers as I walk past him. "Can't be away from you for more than thirty seconds. Maybe we should reschedule that thing we were talking about and do it right now."

Since everyone else is sitting on the sofa or in the armchairs, they couldn't hear what Ben said.

I lean in to kiss his cheek and whisper, "You're on."

The doorbell rings again, then a fist raps on the door. Jeez, whoever that is, they're insanely determined.

I swing the door open.

A woman fixes her sharp gaze on me, eying me up and down like I'm auditioning for a modeling job and she's not too pleased with what she sees. The woman wears what looks like a designer skirt suit, with a fancy gold brooch pinned to the jacket's lapel. She has her honey-blonde hair pinned up in an elaborate bun, and her makeup is flawless. How she managed to walk across the snowy driveway while wearing high heels, I can't imagine.

"I would like to see my son," the woman says. "Now."

Oh yeah, she's got the commanding tone down pat. I feel a bizarre impulse to bow or curtsy or something. Her British accent has me wondering who this elegant, haughty woman is. But I get a wriggly feeling in my gut that warns me I should know the answer.

My dad comes up beside me. "Hey, what's up?"

The woman lifts one manicured brow. "I'm here to retrieve my son. Where is Bennett?"

Oh holy shit. This woman is Ben's mom.

Princess Olivia is standing on my front porch.

Chapter Nineteen

Ben

Where is my son?" a familiar female voice says very loudly from the direction of the front door. My mother continues speaking, but not with as much volume, so I can't understand whatever it is she's saying to Sam and Chuck.

How did Mum find me?

The rest of the Lockharts have started to stare at me, all of them seeming confused to varying degrees. I had told Sam's family about me shortly after her brother arrived with his wife and daughters. Ella and Lily thought it was "so cool" and asked if I have a crown and could they try it on if I did. I don't have a crown, so they were disappointed. But now, even the little girls give me confused looks.

I march over to the front door, where my mother stands just outside the threshold, giving Sam and Chuck her best haughty expression. Of course, being a princess, she also stands with her shoulders rolled back, her spine straight, and her chin slightly lifted. Mum isn't a cold, pretentious royal. She has a softer side, but no one outside the family ever sees it. I haven't seen it in ages—except maybe on the day I ran away. During our conversation on the balcony of my bedroom, right before I sneaked out of the castle, for a moment she'd been the mother I remember instead of the untouchable princess.

Right now, she wants everyone to be intimidated. That might be working on Sam a little bit, but Chuck seems more entertained than cowed.

"So you're Olivia," he says, and thrusts his hand out to her. "It's a real pleasure to meet you. I'm Chuck Lockhart, Sam's dad."

Mum lifts one brow. "Sam? Who on earth is that?"

Chuck nods toward his daughter. "She's Sam. Didn't Ben tell you they're an item?"

Oh bugger. Of course I hadn't told Mum, because I haven't spoken to her or anyone except the Lockharts since I came to New Hampshire. Well, them and the people in town, but they don't know I'm a sodding crown prince. I'd texted my sister, so I hadn't actually spoken to her either.

Princess Olivia of Mithoria rotates her cool gaze toward me. "Bennett, I believe we need to speak in private."

Suddenly, I feel like a little boy again. Only my mother can do that to me.

"Now, Bennett," Mum says in her most authoritative tone.

Chuck's eyebrows draw together. "Uh, maybe we should let you guys have some time alone. We can go into town to buy groceries."

"You guys go on without us," Sam says. "I'm staying with Ben."

Mum aims her coolest stare at my girlfriend.

Sam bites her lip briefly but does not back down. Instead, she squares her shoulders and lifts her chin much the way Mum does. "I love Ben, and I'm staying. Deal with it."

An expression resembling genuine shock flashes on my mother's face, but it vanishes so quickly that I can't be sure I saw it. Princess Olivia is never shocked. She handles every situation, no matter how troubling, with regal composure. Even when she's angry, like she was a moment ago when she commanded me "now, Bennett," she didn't look furious or even annoyed. Her commanding tone is regal too, just like her haughty stare.

I've never had any luck trying to look like that. But today, I need to channel my inner crown prince and become as strong and impenetrable as my mother. I don't mean that she's cold and heartless. She knows how to school her expressions and her demeanor, that's all. I'm ruddy awful at that.

Clasping Sam's hand, I guide her away from the door and wave for Mum to follow us. We move into the living room.

The Lockharts grab their coats and hats and walk out the front door. A moment later, I hear two car engines growl to life. Soon, the noise fades into the distance.

Mum looks at me, then at Sam. She stares at my girlfriend for so long that I'm about to speak up about how rude she's being to Sam. But then Mum whirls on her heels, marches to the front door, and swings it open. She shouts, "Brakefield, get in here. You'll freeze to death out there, you daft fool."

Sam glances at me, her brows raised. She mouths, "Brakefield?"

I lean in to whisper in her ear, "My mother's favorite bodyguard. He goes everywhere with her."

She makes an "O" with her lips and nods.

Mum's right-hand man strides into the house and takes up a position near the kitchen island. The man stands straight and tall, his hands clasped behind his back, and surveys the surroundings without expression.

I'm used to my mother's bodyguards, but Sam seems a bit confused. Before Brakefield, there was Pendergast. Before him, it had been Standish. All of those blokes reminded me of the robot in that old science fiction movie *The Day the Earth Stood Still*. They stand in one place and don't move unless their mistress commands it. They have no expression, and none of them ever spoke to me. When I was a boy, I'd been unsettled by Mum's bodyguards. I'd also wondered why she needed them. No one has ever threatened her life.

Eventually, I realized she uses her bodyguards more like a butler or a chauffeur. I don't think they even carry guns. Wouldn't real bodyguards do that? Not sure. I think Mum calls those gents bodyguards just for show. I've never asked her about that, though.

My mother walks over to the nearest armchair and settles onto it. She folds her hands on her lap, gazing directly at me.

Sam and I sit down on the sofa, side by side.

And Mum's gaze tracks my every movement.

I always start to feel itchy whenever she watches me like that. It means my mother is upset with me, though she will never admit to that. I hold Sam's hand, which makes Mum pucker her lips the faintest bit.

"Who is this girl?" Mum asks. "You never mentioned were dating anyone, and now this child claims to love you."

"I love her too, Mum. This is Samantha Lockhart, and we've been, ah, sort of dating."

"Sort of dating?" She narrows her gaze on me. "If you love her, shouldn't you be formally dating, not 'sort of'?"

Does anyone formally date? That sounds like something that involves chaperons and rules of etiquette. Not that the women Mum threw at me cared about any of that. The last one seemed on the verge of tearing my clothes off just to prove she can satisfy me.

Sam satisfies me in every way, not just with sex.

Mum puckers her lips again. "How long have you known this child?"

"Come off it, Mum. You know bloody well Sam is not a child, and neither am I. We're adults who can make our own decisions." I wrap both hands around Sam's. "We met about a week ago. And before you start telling me how disappointed you are in me, at least get to know Sam. She's a lovely person."

"The girl is American. Couldn't you at least have a fling with a British girl? That's almost Mithorian."

"Sam is not a fling. I am in love with her, Mum. Were you not listening when I said that before?"

"I heard you quite well, Bennett." Mum relaxes her lips, reasserting her cool, calm demeanor. "The jet is waiting for us at the airport. Say goodbye to your bit of skirt and retrieve your luggage. We're going home."

"No."

She jerks backward just a little, her chin tucked. "I must have misheard you. My son would never speak to me that way."

"What way? Oh, you mean the way where I say no instead of tucking my tail between my legs and obeying your commands." I sling an arm around Sam's shoulders, pulling her close. "And she is not a 'bit of skirt.' I've told you I'm in love with her and I'm not leaving, so stop trying to bully me, Mum."

"Bully?" She freezes, her expression going blank.

I have never seen my mother like that. I think she might be…speechless. Maybe that's because I've refused to do what she wants, or maybe it's because I used the word bully. I didn't mean to upset her, but it's time she understood exactly how much I don't want to become the Prince of Mithoria. Not that I have a choice.

Do I?

Before I can consider that question, I need to explain a few things to my mother.

She's still staring at me blankly.

"I'm sorry, Mum," I say. "I know you think you're doing what's best for me, but you don't know me anymore. I never wanted to go to boarding school, but you sent me anyway so I could become a proper crown prince. I hated it. At university, I finally made some friends and started to enjoy my life. Then you tried to make me go back to Mithoria, but I got you to grudgingly agree I could take a few years to enjoy a normal life."

"Yes, I know what happened, Bennett. I was there."

"But I don't think you've ever really listened to me when I told you why I didn't want to go home. I love my job in Cockshire, and I have lots of mates there. Now I've met a woman I could see myself spending the rest of my life with. Don't you want me to be happy, Mum?"

"Of course I do."

"Then why did you drag me home for a months-long parade of avaricious girls? None of them like me. They want to become Princess of Mithoria one day, and they don't care what they have to do to make that happen. The last one tried to shag me on the balcony just to prove she can satisfy my sexual needs."

Mum snaps ramrod straight. "Don't be crude, Bennett. It doesn't befit a crown prince."

"I'm crude? Those girls are the unfit ones, not me. I behaved myself, always, even when I would've rather been back in Cockshire working at Nick's Nirvana. Now that I've found Sam, I will not let you drag me back to Mithoria so I can choose which greedy slag to marry."

"Bennett Worthington Montague, mind your mouth."

"No, I don't think I will. This is the real me, Mum. Maybe it's time you got to know your son, before you abduct me back to the place you call home. And kidnapping is the only way you'll get me to go anywhere with you."

Her mouth falls open.

I've well and truly stunned her this time. Maybe she's long over-due for a dose of reality, but I don't enjoy having a conversation like this with my mother. "I love you, Mum, I do. But you don't know me."

She drops her gaze to her lap, running her fingers over her dress in what seems like nervous movements. "Maybe you have a point. What do you suggest we do?"

Now it's my turn to stare blankly. She wants my opinion? That's never happened before.

"Uh, well…" I struggle to compose a coherent thought, so stunned that my mind is reeling. When Sam squeezes my hand, I glance at her and suddenly feel calmer. I kiss her cheek, then turn to my mother. "Why don't you stay for Christmas? That way you can get to know Sam and me."

"Stay here? In America?"

Yes, she's gaping at me again.

"That's right, Mum. Spend time in America." I smile at her. "Never know, you might make some new friends. Chuck and Judy are lovely people, and I think you'll like them."

"I can't leave your father alone at Christmas."

"So send the jet to bring him here. Have Stephanie come too."

Mum glances around. "This house does not look large enough to accommodate us."

"Buy sleeping bags and camp out on the floor."

Her eyes flare wide, and her face goes pale. "You want the Prince and Princess of Mithoria to camp out on a stranger's floor?"

"If you can't stomach that, Sam and I can take the floor. You and Dad can sleep in our room."

"*Our* room? You're sleeping with her?"

I roll my eyes. "Come on, Mum, you must've realized that earlier. I'm an adult, remember? I can shag whoever I want."

"The crown prince of Mithoria does not behave that way. Or use that word."

"Shag? Lots of people say that. I bet Dad uses that word when he wants to—"

"Enough, Bennett. Crudeness will not convince me to let you do what you want."

Being reasonable isn't working. Trying to appease her isn't either. Maybe I need to take a different approach. "I don't need your permission, Mum. This is my life, and I decide how to live it."

She stares at me without expression for several very long seconds. "I need to speak to Samantha alone, please."

"Mum—"

"Please."

Sam touches my knee. "It's okay. I'm happy to talk to her one on one."

"Are you sure?"

"Yes." She kisses my cheek. "Wait in the bedroom."

While I leave the living room, I glance back several times. But my mother and Sam have not moved or spoken, not yet. Whatever Princess Olivia wants to say to my girlfriend, I know Sam can handle it. She's an amazing woman.

But how will Sam respond if Mum demands she break up with me?

Chapter Twenty

Sam

I'm sitting six feet away from a princess, the wife of the most powerful man in their country. She acts pretty much the way I'd figured a monarch might—regal, commanding, self-assured, and used to getting her way. I can tell she loves her son, and he loves her too. Neither one of them has gotten nasty, and instead, they had an adult discussion. Princess Olivia clearly doesn't like that Ben refuses to do what she says, but she hasn't told him to dump me.

Not yet.

A private conversation with a royal? A woman who seems to disapprove of me? Not sure I'm ready for this, but I'm doing it for Ben.

I fold my hands on my lap. Keep my chin level and my gaze on her. And I wait for her to speak.

"What do you do for a living?" Olivia asks.

"Virtual assistant. That means—"

"I know what it means, dear. We do have the internet in Mithoria." Her lips tighten in a slight smile. "And mobile phones too."

"Sorry, I didn't mean to offend you. When I told my parents about my job, they didn't get it. They do now, but at first, it confused them."

Olivia studies me with her head tipped to the side. "You hardly know my son, yet you claim to love him."

"I do know him. Ben and I have talked a lot, and I feel closer to him than I do with my family. We've shared everything with each other, and I've never had that kind of intimacy before. It's wonderful."

Maybe I shouldn't have blabbed all of that to her. What if she thinks I'm an idiot? Will she actually abduct Ben back to Mithoria?

Olivia leans back in her chair, crossing her legs. "What would you do if I ordered you to end your relationship with my son?"

"I would say hell no."

Yeah, I'd thought about saying something more diplomatic, but I think she's testing me. I need to show her who I really am, so she'll understand that I won't let her take Ben away from me without a fight. I realize I risk offending her with this tactic, but I need to be honest.

She raises her brows. "You do realize you're speaking to the second-highest ranking member of the Mithorian royal family."

"Isn't your family just you, your husband, Ben, and his sister?"

"Yes." She rests her hands on the chair's arms and slowly taps one finger. "What would you sacrifice to be with Bennett?"

"Anything. I love him."

"Bennett is a crown prince. You are not even an aristocrat."

I just stifle a snort of laughter. "We don't have royalty or aristocracy in America. Status and titles aren't important to me. I love Ben for who he is, not how much money and power he might have."

"He has no power at the moment, since he has not ascended the throne yet. And his allowance has been withheld indefinitely."

"Because you're punishing him for wanting to decide for himself how to live his life."

She steeples her fingers under her chin while keeping her elbows on the chair's arms. "I can already tell you are not a wallflower. You have strength of spirit."

"Uh, thank you." Was that a compliment or some kind of sneaky dig? I can't tell for sure. This woman hasn't given me any clues to help me deduce what her goal is. Does she want to chase me away? Or size me up? Maybe both.

"Tell me how you met Bennett," Olivia says.

So I tell her, though I leave out the part where Ben and I gave each other orgasms on the sofa bed. I think her face might turn crimson and steam might erupt from her ears if I share that tidbit. Once I've finished the story, Olivia just keeps watching me.

Her bodyguard-slash-chauffeur, Brakefield, has been standing near the kitchen island the whole time. He must've overheard everything we said, but he wears a stony expression and gazes out the windows instead of looking at us.

"Thank you for keeping Bennett safe," Olivia says at last.

"Anybody would've done the same thing."

"Even so, what you did was brave."

I feel a strange urge to hunch my shoulders, like I'm embarrassed or something. Maybe her compliment does make me feel that way, just a touch. I don't think it was brave to rescue Ben. I wasn't in any danger.

Olivia sits forward and clears her throat. "I can tell you're quite fond of Ben, and he cares for you too. That means I should get to know you. But this house is not large enough to accommodate all of us."

"What are you saying?"

"Come back to Mithoria with us. Spend Christmas there. Your family is, of course, welcome to come along."

Am I hallucinating? Did a princess just invite me to spend the holidays in her country? I need a little clarification on that offer. "Where exactly would my family and I stay?"

Her mouth relaxes, though she doesn't quite smile. "In the castle, dear. Though for the sake of appearances, you and Bennett should sleep in separate rooms."

She didn't order me not to have sex with him. And I'd bet Ben knows how to sneak me into his bedroom. He told me he's never had a girl in his room back in Mithoria, but he did escape from the castle. He must know secret routes inside the building.

Am I seriously considering accepting her offer? I did say I would do anything for Ben. And I meant it.

"Let's do it," I say. "Let's go to Mithoria. It would be great to see where Ben comes from and to meet the rest of your family."

Princess Olivia stops blinking. Her gaze remains locked on me, but her lips fall open a tiny bit, just enough to convey the fact she clearly did not expect me to agree to her proposal. But she reasserts her royal demeanor within a few seconds. "I'm pleased that you have agreed, and I'm sure Bennett will be pleased as well. You should see Mithoria, and see how we live, before you become too deeply involved with my son."

Too late for that. I'm all in right now.

"I appreciate your invitation," I say. "And I'm excited to visit Mithoria. But before we go there, maybe I could show you my world. New Hampshire is beautiful, and the people are so nice."

"How long would you like me to remain here?"

"A couple of days ought to do it."

She purses her lips faintly, gazing out the window. Then she looks straight at me. "All right. I will remain here for two days and experience New Hampshire."

Despite the fact she speaks the name of this state like it feels uncomfortable on her tongue, I think she honestly wants to explore this area. Ben seems to like it here, so I'm sure his mom wants to understand why. I've known Olivia Montague for maybe twenty minutes, but somehow I can tell that about her.

Besides, I have a new mantra—anything for Ben.

Princess Olivia glances over her shoulder at the stoic man beside the island. "Brakefield, please fetch my son."

"Allow me," I say. Then I twist around to holler toward the hallway, "Ben! You can come back out here."

Olivia's mouth twists into a partial smile.

Ben emerges from the bedroom and trots over to the sofa, halting behind it—behind me. He bends to kiss the top of my head, then smirks at his mother. "Well, Mum isn't turning purple, so I guess the chat went all right."

"It went great," I say. "Your mom and I came up with a plan."

"A plan? Do I want to know?"

"Yes, Bennett," Olivia says. "You do want to know."

"What is the plan?"

"You and Samantha will come home to Mithoria for Christmas. But first, I will spend two days here in New Hampshire finding out why this place has entranced you."

"It's not the place, Mum." He lays his hands on my shoulders. "It's the woman."

A warm, glowy feeling spreads through my chest. I lay my hands over his and try not to smile like a lovestruck idiot. All Ben said was that he's stayed in New Hampshire because of me, not because of the scenery. But that simple declaration makes me feel almost euphoric.

"Why don't we start today?" I ask Olivia. "Unless you're too wiped out from the plane ride."

"I do not get 'wiped out', dear. Indeed we should start today."

She stands up like she's about to head for the front door.

"You might want to change clothes," I say. "It's cold out there, and nobody in North Slipperton wears designer duds. You look amazing, don't get me wrong."

"North Slipperton?" she says like I've spoken an alien language.

Ben squeezes my shoulders as he tells his mother, "That's the name of the nearest town, Mum. It's a nice place. They have a store too, where you could buy a snowsuit."

"A snow what?"

"Suit. It's what everybody wears around here in the winter. The suit will keep you warm."

"What sort of store sells such things?"

"It's called the Discount Depot."

Her lip curls, but she flattens it out quickly. "Thank you for the suggestion, but I do not shop at any establishment that includes the word discount in its name."

"Don't be a snob, Mum. Give it a go. At least go inside the store before you turn your nose up at it."

"It's a cool place," I say. "Never know, you might decide 'discount' isn't a dirty word."

"That's right," Ben agrees. "Sam and I love that store and the whole town. Hartmoor is great too, but it's a bit further away."

Olivia looks at her son, then me, then she shuts her eyes for a moment. When she opens them again, she sighs and sags her shoulders. "All right. I will visit this Discount Depot. Please tell me there is at least a good restaurant in town."

Ben grins. "Sure there is. It's called the Crab Cottage."

Did Olivia just go pale? I think she might have, though not enough that I can tell for sure. The Crab Cottage might not be a five-star restaurant, but it has good food. Though maybe we shouldn't take Ben's mom there since we had sex in that place.

It's the only restaurant in town. I'll just have to try not to think about how I mounted Ben in one of the booths.

"Let me call my mom," I say, "and alert them that we're coming into town. We can all meet up at the Discount Depot, then go out for dinner."

"Sounds perfect," Ben says.

Olivia flattens her lips into a line. "Yes, it sounds wonderful."

No, she didn't say that with any sincerity. She sounded defeated.

Will Princess Olivia ever accept me? I don't care about that. Only one thing matters. Will Ben stay with me even if his family disapproves?

Chapter Twenty-One

Ben

The Lockhart women have decided to show my mother what normal life is like for normal people. Yeah, that's going to lead to a meltdown of nuclear proportions, for sure. I love Mum, but she can be a bit of a snob sometimes. She married Dad at age twenty-one and became a princess three years later, so Mum has spent decades perfecting her royal attitude. I think she also built a shell around herself as protection against the inevitable verbal attacks. We did have a few instances of physical attacks, but they involved eggs thrown at my parents or toilet paper strewn over the trees outside the castle. None of us were in any real danger. It was teenagers having a lark.

I can vaguely remember when I was little and my mum and dad used to play silly games with me. My sister Stephanie probably doesn't remember much of that since she's four years younger than I am. But I can still picture those days, before my parents got so caught up in being royal that they forgot how to have fun, even in private. When I was fourteen, I asked my mother why she'd gotten so uptight—yes, even royal teenage boys say stupid things like that—and I can still picture the look on her face. Lips tight. Eyes narrowed. The expression lasted only a second, two at most, before she reasserted her usual calm demeanor.

"A princess must be on guard every moment," she told me, "or the vultures will swoop in. We are more than figureheads. We *are* the nation of Mithoria, your father and I, and we must always be seen as sober and in command. You'll understand this when you're older, Bennett."

I do understand now, but I don't want to live the way she and Dad do.

The first stage of the Lockhart women's plan for my mother involves convincing her to buy a snowsuit and a flannel shirt. Princess Olivia in flannel? Not bloody likely. Mum will dress goth before she tries flannel of any sort. That's the snob's equivalent of wearing dirty clothes. I'm wearing a flannel shirt, though, and it's very comfortable. Sam bought me this shirt the other day. I put it on after Mum arrived, while she was having her chat with Sam. Waiting for the women to finish their discussion left me with nothing to do while I hid in the bedroom, and I couldn't resist walking out into the living room while wearing plaid flannel.

Mum's eyes bulged when she saw me. I swear they did.

She doesn't mind jeans, though she has told me many times that I'm "too old to dress that way." I asked what way she meant, but she just sniffed and puckered her lips.

I still wear jeans. Whenever I bloody well feel like it. And now I wear plaid flannel too.

Mum relaxes a bit on the drive into town, but when she sees the sign for the Discount Depot, I can tell she's struggling not to pucker her lips or say something snobby about the store. To her credit, she does not complain. She does, however, wait for Brakefield to open the car door for her and hold her hand to help her get out. I do the same for Sam. I would've helped Mum too, but she prefers to have Brakefield do it. Something about boundaries and propriety, or maybe I have clammy palms and that's why she never wants to touch my hand.

Sam kisses my cheek when I help her out of the car.

Mum does not kiss Brakefield's cheek. I think the bloke might run away in terror if she did that.

Inside the store, we find Sam's family already waiting for us. They're browsing the plastic bins that hold various knickknacks, like bobblehead toys and teddy bear key chains. Yes, I can envision Mum unlocking the castle door with one of those key chains and keeping her collection of bobblehead leprechauns on the sitting room mantel.

Sam introduces her family to Mum, and they're all thrilled to meet her, though not because she's a princess. Ella sums it up the best when she says, "We're sooo happy to meet you, Princess Olivia. Ben is super nice, and we knew you would be too."

I'm super nice? Maybe an endorsement from a ten-year-old shouldn't make me happy, but embarrassingly, it does.

Mum might not appreciate the simpler things in life, but she's always kind to children. She kneels to speak to eight-year-old Lily, offering a friendly smile. "You are as beautiful as any princess, and I'm very pleased to meet you, dear."

Yes, my mother can be nice. I've known that all my life, but I miss the days when she was always like this.

After the introductions are over, Chuck tosses a flannel shirt to my mother. "Try this on for size, Ollie."

Did he just call my mother, the Princess of Mithoria, Ollie? Yeah, he did. And I kind of love Chuck for doing that. I might even smack a wet one on his cheek.

My mother catches the shirt, lifting one brow. "Do you have one in blue?"

"Sure thing." Chuck grabs another shirt and tosses it to her. "Try this one."

"Thank you, Mr. Lockhart."

"Call me Chuck. We're kinda almost family now, aren't we?"

Mum glances at me. "I suppose we are."

For a moment, I can't move or speak. Just as I feel like I'm regaining my motor and brain functions, my mother slips a flannel shirt on over her dress and buttons it up, then she twirls to let us all see her ensemble—a designer dress and designer high heels with a flannel shirt from a discount store.

I think I've just had a stroke. Or a heart attack. Maybe it's just a panic attack since I have never seen my mother wear anything as ordinary as flannel, never in my entire life. First, she implies that Sam might join our family, then she does this. Did Chuck slip her some marijuana? I can't see any other explanation for Mum's behavior right now. It reminds me of the way she used to be when I was younger.

Next, the Lockharts help Princess Olivia choose the right snow-suit, which they insist she'll need when we all go snowmobiling.

My mother on a snowmobile? Good thing Brakefield decided to wait in the car. He'd go apoplectic if he heard someone suggest the princess would do anything as dangerous as that.

But Mum says, "That sounds like fun."

And yes, the next day my mother rides a snowmobile while wearing a white snowsuit and a knit cap with matching gloves, not to mention goggles. She doesn't drive the machine. Chuck does that so Mum can enjoy the ride. Oh yeah, she enjoys it all right. Princess Olivia whoops as she and Chuck race down the mountainside.

While Sam and I watch from a safe distance, she says, "I thought your mother was rigid and proper. That's how you described her, and that's kind of how she acted yesterday when she first arrived."

"I haven't seen Mum act this way in years. She doesn't drive a car herself, much less jump on a snowmobile and whoop so loudly it echoes off the trees." I shake my head, staring down the hill with my mouth gaping open as Chuck spins the snowmobile around and they rocket back toward us. "Mum won't let Brakefield drive faster than fifty miles an hour."

Sam laughs. "I think Dad's driving a little faster than that."

Chuck stops the machine so suddenly that snow sprays up. Then he hops off and helps Mum get off the snowmobile too.

"How'd you like it?" Judy asks. "Fun, hey?"

"Bloody fantastic," Mum says while grinning.

My mother just said the word bloody, and she wasn't talking about how she likes her ribeye steak. Not that Mum eats steak. She's also grinning.

"Who wants some hot cocoa?" Cameron asks.

Ella and Lily jump up and down. "Me! Me!"

"Me too," Mum says, and she grins again.

Once we all get inside the cabin, I take my mother over to the farthest corner of the living room. "Are you feeling all right, Mum?"

"Fabulous, darling." She kisses my cheek. "Haven't had this much fun in years. Almost forgot what it feels like to cut loose. You and Sam and her family have given me a much-needed refresher course in enjoying life."

"But you rode a snowmobile. And last night, you slept in a sleeping bag. On the floor. In the living room with Cameron, Amy, and their daughters."

"I braided the girls' hair too."

"You did what?" I am genuinely gaping, and I'm positive my jaw has dropped low enough that it will graze my chest if I try to speak.

My mother lays a hand on my shoulder. "Don't look so stunned, darling. We used to have fun all the time."

"When I was little. Once I left for boarding school, everything changed."

"Exactly." Her smile fades, and she moves her hand to my cheek. "I missed you, Ben. Honestly, I didn't want to send you away, but that's how it's always been done in the Montague family. It seemed like the right thing at the time, but I regret it now."

"It's all right. Boarding school wasn't so awful. And I loved going to university."

"We do need to get to know each other again. I want to do that." She pulls me into a hug. "I love you, Ben, and I want you to be happy."

"I love you too, Mum. And I am happy."

She lets go of me. "But not when you're in Mithoria."

"Well, it's, ah…"

"You don't need to placate me, dear. I know you've never wanted to rule the country. You love your job in England and your friends there."

"I love Sam too."

"Yes, I know." She sighs, all the happiness vanishing from her expression. "I will do whatever it takes to make my children happy."

"Stephanie is happy. She loves all that royal rubbish."

"That's true." Mum gets a look on her face that I know well. It means she's plotting something. After a moment, though, she smiles. "Let's not worry about anything right now. It's Christmastime, and we are all about to fly to Mithoria for the holidays."

And that's what we do. An hour after my mother spoke those words, the lot of us head for the airport where the Mithorian royal jet is waiting for us. It doesn't say "Mithorian royal jet" on the side of the aircraft. It's just plain white.

In a matter of hours, we touch down on the island nation of Mithoria.

We don't get much snow here, so Ella and Lily are slightly disappointed they won't have a white Christmas, but they forget about that once they see the castle. The royal residence seems tiny in comparison to Buckingham Palace or Versailles, but it's nothing to sneeze at either. Montague Castle sits atop the highest hill on the island, its turrets rising into the sky and its flags waving in the wind. The structure looks like something out of a fairy tale, with rounded turrets that have round roofs, and a wall that surrounds the compound, as well as massive wooden gates.

We all managed to fit inside a long limousine—driven by Brakefield, of course. As we roll up the paved road that leads to the gates, Lily and Ella get so excited that Cameron and Amy have to hold them down so they won't leap out the window. No joke. They wanted to climb out and run to the gateway.

"It's just like Cinderella's castle," Lily says. "Are you Prince Charming, Ben?"

"Uh, no. I'm not a prince yet, anyway. I'm the crown prince, which means—"

"Look! Look!" Ella shouts. "I see horses!"

Yes, we do have a horse stable just outside the castle walls. Montagues have always owned horses, and we still keep several on the premises. Only my sister Stephanie rides these days, but sometimes guests want to explore the area by horseback.

The gates are open, waiting for us to arrive. People are waiting for us too. The entire staff has lined up along either side of the courtyard, and my father and sister plus her fiancé, Wesley, wait there too.

Brakefield parks the car in the courtyard.

Ella and Lily want to leap out immediately, but we have ruddy rules about the etiquette of exiting a vehicle. We all wait while Brakefield gets out and opens the door for us. My mother steps out first, followed by me—as etiquette requires. It's bollocks, but I go along with it because I never want to embarrass my family. They believe in decorum, while I'm a massage therapist who has sex in hot tubs.

Once everyone has gotten out of the car, Mum leads us toward Dad and Stephanie.

And the spectacle begins.

Chapter Twenty-Two

Sam

I have never experienced this much pageantry in my life. It all goes by in a big blur of waving flags and trumpet fanfares as we walk up a crimson carpet to join the other Montagues. Soldiers holding what I think are ceremonial rifles perform a routine while Princess Olivia takes her place at Prince Leighton's side. As crown prince, Ben stands beside his mother with his sister on his other side. My family and I are encouraged to take up positions behind the royal family.

After some more pageantry, we're guided into the castle.

Maybe I'd hoped for a grand tour of the place, but instead, we're led to our assigned quarters. Yeah, those are the exact words Olivia uses. Ben has the second largest room in the castle, while his sister gets the third largest. Their parents have the "royal chambers" on the top floor. Ben and Stephanie have their own "royal chambers" on the floor just below where their parents sleep. The rest of us are on the floor below the crown prince and his sister, whatever title she has. I didn't catch it if somebody announced her title, or maybe she doesn't have one.

This is all so confusing and overwhelming. My room in Montague Castle is bigger than my entire house back home.

For the next several days, I don't get to spend much time with Ben. He has official duties to uphold, like judging a Christmas ornament competition. The people of Mithoria compete to craft the most beautiful handmade ornaments, and I don't know how he can choose just one. They're all gorgeous. I get pulled into some events too, like Princess Olivia's holiday stroll through the village that lies at the base of the mountain atop which Montague Castle sits. Olivia doesn't just walk by while giving everyone the royal wave. She stops to talk to people, and they clearly love her—not only as their princess, but as just a woman too.

When I do see Ben, it's at public gatherings or during family dinners.

Two days before Christmas, I can't stand it anymore. I need some alone time with my boyfriend, if only to feel his arms around me again. So I do something naughty. I sneak upstairs after everyone has gone to bed and all the lights are off, except for the night lights positioned in every corridor, and I carefully open the door to Ben's bedroom. Once I've slipped inside, I ease the door shut.

A light pops on, spilling its warm golden light through the room.

Ben lies in bed, shirtless, propped up with two pillows. "I was hoping you'd sneak into my room sometime."

"Couldn't wait any longer. I miss you."

"I miss you too." He flips the covers off himself, revealing the fact he's buck naked. "Get your sexy arse over here."

I hurry to the bed and climb onto it, kneeling beside him.

"Never had a woman in this bed before," he says as he moves to crouch near the foot of the bed. "Lie down, please. I need to make love to you."

Do I hesitate? Of course not. I shimmy over to lie down where he had been a moment ago. The bed still feels warm from his body.

"Your nightie," he says.

I strip it off and toss the lacy garment onto the floor. "Ready to go."

Ben settles his hands on my feet and glides them over my ankles, up my calves. His warm palms feel so good on my skin, and a sultry tingle sweeps over me from head to toe as anticipation makes my breaths heavier. We haven't been alone, completely alone, in several days that seemed like forever. I love being with him even when we're fully clothed and can't touch each other in sexy ways, but I need to feel him inside me tonight.

"I am a massage therapist, you know," he says, his voice so deep and sensual that my clit throbs. "That means I know every way to touch you and get you so turned on that you'll beg me to fuck you."

"Don't need to wait for that. Please, Ben, make love to me now, please."

His lips slide into a wicked smile. "I love your enthusiasm, but I have plans for your body. Plans that will take time."

"Take as long as you want, just keep touching me."

"I will, that's a promise."

He starts to massage my flesh, starting near my knee and making his way back down to my feet. When he slides his fingers onto my soles and rubs with his thumbs, I can't help moaning. No other guy I've dated wanted to rub my feet, much less rub me down from head to toe like I know Ben wants to do. He massages a path back up my calves while he curls his fingers around them to work every muscle, not just the exposed sides. His touch is delicate at first, then his fingers sink in deep to loosen every knot and tight spot.

"How did I get so lucky?" I ask. "Rescuing a hot Brit who's also a massage therapist."

"Guess you've been a very good girl." He smirks as he skims his palms over my knees. "Or a very naughty one. Both, I'd say."

"Mm, Ben, keep touching me this way. I love it."

"Anything for you, love."

He skates his palms over my belly, teasing my navel with one finger, and moves his hands up to gently massage my breasts. With his deft thumbs, he rubs in circles around my stiff nipples, coming within millimeters of those taut peaks, only to withdraw his fingers. I arch my back and moan again while I clench the sheets. He slides his hands under my neck, delicately rubbing the muscles at my nape, and pushes his fingers into my hair to cradle my head. His face hovers so close to mine that I can feel his breaths whispering over my skin.

I also feel his erection brushing over my belly.

He grazes his lips across mine. "Should I massage your backside too? Or move on to the main event."

"Main event, please. I can't wait any longer."

Ben presses his lips to mine, softly at first, the pressure increasing every second until his mouth is crushed to mine. He thrusts his tongue between my lips, exploring with leisurely movements while

I tunnel my fingers into his hair and bend my knees, all but begging him to take me. He gives up my mouth to kiss a trail down my throat while he shimmies down my body, the hard line of his cock scraping over my flesh. He pauses with his face hovering over my mound and peeks up at me through his thick lashes.

Then he pushes his mouth between my folds.

I gasp when he drags his tongue down one side and back up the other, not just once, but three times. When he lifts his head to look at me, his lips glisten with my wetness, and his nose does too. I can't help giggling when I see that. He smirks and rubs his nose into my clitoris, then drags his tongue down the center of my cleft to dive it inside my opening and swirl the tip.

"Oh, yes, Ben," I cry out while my fingers clench the sheets even harder.

He latches on to my clit and suckles it.

I come in an instant, my body taut while waves of pleasure crash through me. I suddenly realize someone might hear my noises, and I try not to cry out again, but I can't stop it from happening. My cries echo off the walls of this huge bedroom while Ben keeps suckling and licking my nub until I go limp on the bed.

He raises onto his hands and knees. "Hand me a condom, love. They're in the top drawer of the nightstand."

I somehow manage to understand his words and make my muscles move so I can retrieve a foil packet from the nightstand. Luckily, I don't need to do more than fling my arm out to open the drawer on the little table beside the bed. Not sure I could've moved any more than that if I tried. But I grab the packet and hand it to Ben.

He rolls the condom on and crouches over me with his head above mine. "I love you, Sam, and I never want to be without you."

"I love you too, Ben, so much."

"Spread your legs for me, pet."

As soon as I part my thighs for him, he pulls his hips back and plunges inside me. I grip his biceps while he thrusts in and out, taking his time, gliding in deep only to glide back out again until only the head of his cock is inside me. It feels so good that I can barely catch my breath, and I instinctively wrap my legs around his hips to let him dive even deeper into my body. He drops onto his elbows, his head nestled against my neck and his breaths blustering over my skin.

I lash my arms around him and hold on for the ride.

He thrusts faster and harder as the bed begins to shake and creak. But when he raises onto his straight arms and punches into me with even more force, the bed thumps so loudly that it echoes inside the room and I'm positive whoever has the room under us can hear what's going on in the crown prince's bedroom. I don't care who hears us. The tension rises inside me, building like a boiling pot with a lid clamped over it, and I know soon that steam will blow my top.

Ben has his face scrunched up in a combination of pleasure and agony, and I know he's about to blow his top too.

I go first, my inner muscles squeezing him over and over while the orgasm fires down my nerves straight into my clit. I cling to him and scream his name. He reaches down to rub my still-rigid nub, scorching new and hotter pleasure through me while I cry out again. He pounds into me three more times, shouting my name while he throws his head back.

Ben lies down beside me, breathing hard.

I roll over to sprawl half over his body, drawing invisible circles on his chest with my finger. "That was amazing."

"Yeah, it was." He kisses the top of my head. "I finally seduced a girl in my royal quarters."

"Everybody probably heard us."

"I doubt it. The walls and floors are thick. But even if someone heard us, I don't care. Do you?"

"No. When I'm with you, I don't care what anyone else thinks."

He folds his arms around me. "Tomorrow is Christmas Eve. That means we will participate in the royal procession through town."

"We? I'm not a member of the royal family, so you must've meant 'we' as in you and your parents and Stephanie."

"No, I meant you." He hooks a finger under my chin, encouraging me to look up at him. "I want you by my side during the procession. Is that all right?"

"Yes. Of course I'll be there with you."

"Good," he says with a sigh, almost as if he was worried I might say no. "There's one more thing I need to ask you."

"Okay."

He wriggles out from under me and sits up, leaning over my body to get something out of the second drawer on the nightstand. When he kneels on the bed, I can see he's holding something in his hand, but I can't tell what it is because he closed his fist around it. "Maybe this isn't the most romantic way to do this, but I can't wait any longer."

"You can't wait for what?"

Ben sits back on his heels and waves his hand. "Get up, please.

I push myself up and kneel in front of him. "Ready."

He clears his throat and holds out the little box, flipping up the lid. "Samantha Lockhart, will you marry me?"

Yeah, he's got a diamond ring in that velvet box.

For a second, I'm so stunned that I can't speak to respond to his question. Then a grin stretches my lips. "Yes, of course I'll marry you, Ben."

He grins too. "You will? Even though my life is crazy and my family lives in a ruddy castle?"

"Don't care what your family does. You mean the world to me, Ben, and I want to spend the rest of my life with you."

He slips the ring onto my finger, tosses the box away, and drags me back down onto the bed. For the next hour, we make love and play and laugh until neither of us can keep our eyes open. Then we fall asleep tangled up in each other's arms.

Who knew a snowstorm would change my life forever?

Chapter Twenty-Three

Ben

*I*s there a better way to wake up in the morning than lying in bed with Sam draped over me? The answer is no. Nothing compares to this. Not only is she in my bed, naked and tousled, but she's also the first woman I've ever invited into this room, much less shagged in my "royal quarters." I've always thought that was a bloody stupid name for my bedroom. It sounds medieval, and I am a modern crown prince, not some arsehole who kidnaps women and forces them to marry me or become my sex slaves.

But Sam *is* marrying me. She said yes.

Those greedy girls can find another poor sod to harass. I'm taken.

Although I love watching Sam sleep, I wake her up so we can both get dressed for breakfast. That means she has to hurry downstairs to her assigned bedroom, where she left all her belongings. I don't see her again until I walk into the dining room on the first floor. My parents are there already, as are Stephanie and her fiancé, Wesley, and Brakefield too.

When I sit down beside Sam, she whispers in my ear, "Isn't it strange for a bodyguard to eat with the royal family?"

"You've seen Brakefield eat with us every day. Now you finally ask that question?"

"I wasn't engaged to you before, so I didn't feel it was my place to ask."

"Ah, I see. You asked plenty of impertinent questions all week, but the topic of my mother's bodyguard made you uncomfortable."

"I wasn't impertinent. I was curious."

"Yes, that explains everything." I cast her a sideways glance, and I might be smirking. "For your information, Brakefield resisted the idea of eating with us. But Mum is persistent and persuasive. He finally gave in."

"Why did she want him to eat with you guys so badly?"

"Because she likes him. He's not much older than I am, so Brakefield is kind of like a son to Mum."

"Does that bother you?"

I shrug. "Why should it? I'm not a snob, you know."

"Never thought you were. But he's not a family member."

"To Mum, he is. And we all want her to be happy."

My response seems to satisfy her, and we don't talk any more once the food is served.

That afternoon, it's time for the royal procession to celebrate Christmas Eve. I hold Sam's hand while we amble down the main street in the village, waving to the people gathered along either side. Sam was surprised when I told her we don't dress up for this event, at least not in the "crazy spiffy" way she tells me she expected. Dad and I wear suits and ties, while Mum and Stephanie wear nice dresses, though their frocks aren't designer items. Neither are the suits Dad and I wear. Wesley, Stephanie's fiancé, is dressed in the same way. We all stop occasionally to shake hands with the townsfolk, chat to them, and even kiss a few babies. It's informal, which explains why Sam was surprised. Most of the other events this week have been full of the pageantry she expected.

The procession ends at the only church in this town, where Mum and Dad turn on the lights on the village Christmas tree right before we all file into the chapel for services. After that, we lead the entire town in singing carols in front of the big tree.

We have dinner at home, as a family, though our "home" is an enormous castle. Then we open our presents in the sitting room with a fire roaring in the hearth. What we gave each other hardly matters. It's the fact we're together that means everything, especially now that I have Sam in my life. When we announce our engagement the next morning, everyone is thrilled. Maybe I had worried a little that my mother might not approve, but I was wrong. She hugs Sam and tells her to "call me Mum, darling."

Christmas dinner is a feast for sure. Sam can't believe how many dishes are served, or that we have a three-course meal along with appetizers and dessert too.

The biggest surprise comes that evening when Mum asks me and Sam to meet her in her office. Yes, my mother has an office inside the castle. So does Dad, but that's no surprise. He is the Prince of Mithoria, after all. Mum's office isn't quite as large as Dad's, but it's still bigger than the living room in Sam's cabin.

Mum waits for us behind her desk, waving for Sam and me to take the chairs on the other side. Princess Olivia sits regally straight with her hands folded on the desktop. "Leighton and I have discussed the issue of Bennett's future, and we've come to a decision."

"I'm an adult, Mum. I can make my own decisions."

"Don't get cheeky with me, Ben, or I might change my mind." She's almost smiling when she says that, so I know she won't reverse whatever decision my parents have made together.

I glance at Sam, and she raises her brows. I shrug.

"Leighton and I agree," my mother says, "that you should not become Prince of Mithoria unless that's what you truly want. Your father intends to live to a ripe old age, but we don't want you to be miserable worrying about the day when you'll need to take over as prince. So, the question is simple. Do you want to give up being the crown prince and lead a relatively normal life in England?"

"Are you serious? How can I do that? Who would become the crown prince in my place?"

"Your sister will become the crown princess."

"But a woman can't rule Mithoria. This is a principality, which means a prince is in charge. That's what you've always told me. Besides, I'm the oldest child."

Mum leans back in her chair and gives me a mischievous smile, the sort I've never seen from her before. "Times have changed, darling. And so has Mithoria. Leighton and I have explored the legality of this issue. While the original charter for Mithoria declared a prince would always reign, it left, shall we say, wiggle room. The parliament voted on the issue earlier this week, though their approval wasn't strictly required."

"I didn't hear anything about a vote."

"No one pays attention to parliament. The point is, if you no longer wish to be the crown prince, you may give it up."

"Why would you do this?"

She walks around the desk to kneel beside my chair and lays a hand on my arm. "I did this because I love you, Ben. I want my son to be happy, but I've spent so long trying to mold you into the perfect prince that I forgot to take care of *you*. Spending time with you and Sam in New Hampshire helped me remember what I used to be like before I let the royal lifestyle consume me. Please forgive me for pushing all those horrible women at you. I thought I was doing the right thing, but now I realize I was doing the opposite."

"There's nothing to apologize for. You thought it was the right thing."

"But I was terribly wrong, about everything. I know your true home is in England. You have a job and friends there."

"My true home will always be Mithoria. But yeah, I love my life in England."

"Then you can give up being the crown prince. Say the word, and your father and I will handle everything. Your trust fund has already been reopened, for you to use as often as you like."

I can't speak or move, my gaze glued to my mother. She just told me I can have the life I want, but suddenly, I feel odd about not being the crown prince anymore. I'll still be a member of the royal family, though. I need to know how Sam feels about this first. So I turn toward her. "Would you want to live with me in England? I know your family is in America—"

Mum speaks before Sam has a chance. "You two may borrow the royal jet whenever you like. We can send it to pick up your family too, Sam, so they can visit you in England."

I glance at Mum, then aim my gaze once again at the woman I love.

"Yes," Sam says. "I would love to live with you anywhere. England sounds awesome."

And that's how my life changed forever. The transformation began on the night when Sam rescued me from a blizzard, but I would still be the crown prince if my mother hadn't done something that used to be unthinkable. She set me free. I don't think I can ever properly thank my parents and my sister for giving me the freedom I've wanted for so long.

Mum says all the thanks she needs are grandchildren.

Sam and I agree we can definitely fulfill that request. And yeah, we start working on it that very night—my last night as the crown prince of Mithoria. In the morning, we leave for England.

But the adventure isn't over quite yet.

Cockshire, England
Three Months Later

I'm relaxing on a lawn chaise this afternoon, enjoying a beautiful summer's day in the village that has become my home and Sam's. She relaxes on a chaise too, but she's wearing only a bikini top and very short shorts while I have on normal shorts and a T-shirt. I can't resist raking my gaze over her entire body, which I've done several times in the last few minutes, ever since we sat down here.

This is our backyard. Behind our house. We've been married for exactly two weeks, three days, one hour, and forty-six minutes. Yeah, I just checked my watch to be sure. My beautiful, sexy, clever, wonderful wife lies two feet away from me with a contented smile curving her lips.

Eighties pop music plays through the speakers Nick Hunter had set up on the patio, though Reese Dixon chose the genre we would all be subjected to this afternoon. His wife, Arden, is obsessed with those cheesy songs from the eighties, and we all decided to let her have at it. Arden is currently dancing with Reese to a song I don't remember the name of, but it's actually quite a fun one that makes me want to get up and dance. I used to hate doing that, but something about marrying my dream girl has loosened me up. Not that I was uptight before. Sam says I've gotten "even better and hotter in every way."

Well, I can live with that description.

My clients at the spa are happy I'm home again. Nick even threw a "welcome back to Nirvana" party for me on my first day back at work, which was three days after Sam and I left Mithoria. She still does her virtual assistant thing, but now she works from the house we bought in Cockshire a week after my return. Both our families flew to England on the royal jet for our wedding, though they had already visited us twice on weekend excursions before that. Mum has developed motherly crushes on all my mates, but none of them seem to mind. Neither do the women in their lives.

Sam stretches her entire body and sighs with deep satisfaction. "This is a great party. But who's that guy over there? I don't recognize him. He must not have been at the wedding."

"Oh, he was. But you were overwhelmed by all the Mithorians in attendance, and I didn't get a chance to introduce you to him. Besides, he slipped away with a lady friend halfway through the reception."

My wife sits up and swings her feet off the chaise. "Introduce me now. I'm dying to meet the mystery man."

"All right. But there's no mystery."

"For me, there is."

I get up and take my wife's hand, leading her toward the one man she hasn't met yet. He's just finished chatting to Siobhan Hunter, Nick's wife, and she flashes us a smile as she heads off to find her husband.

"There you are, mate," I say as we approach the bloke in question. "My wife wants to meet you. She thinks you're mysterious, but the rest of us know you're just a chancer with an oversize libido."

I only say things like that because he knows I'm joking. Well, mostly joking. There is some truth to what I said.

My mate smirks. "I can't deny that assessment. But how did shy Ben get himself a gorgeous girl?"

Sam glances back and forth between us, her brows crinkled in the most adorable way.

I nod toward my mate. "Sam, this is Hugh Parrish, also known as Lord Steamy."

Hugh makes a disgusted noise. "Come off it, Ben. Nobody who knows me calls me that."

"Sure we do. I heard Chance tell Elena that's your official title."

My wife seems even more confused. "Lord Steamy?"

Hugh rolls his eyes. "That's not a real title. It's what silly birds call me because they're...silly birds."

"He means girls," I tell Sam. "He's a viscount."

"A what?" she says. "Is that like Count Dracula?"

"No, but I've heard rumors about Hugh and a pair of plastic fangs…"

"Don't believe every rumor you hear," Hugh says. Then he offers his hand to Sam. "May I formally introduce myself? I am Hugh Parrish, Viscount of Sommerleigh. And a viscount is not a vampire. It's a title just below earl but above baron."

Same shakes his hand. "Nice to meet you, Lord… What should I call you?"

"I prefer Hugh. But if you insist on formality, I'm Lord Sommerleigh."

"Well, Hugh, I'm Samantha Montague. But you can call me Sam."

He winks at me. "I'm sure Ben calls you all sorts of other things."

My wife ignores that comment. "So, you must be a real ladies' man to be called Lord Steamy."

"Oh yes, I am world famous."

I shake my head. "Infamous is more like it. How many times have you been caught sneaking into a proper English lady's boudoir and gotten horse-whipped for it?"

"Very funny. I've never been whipped." He smirks. "Though I have had girls beg me to whip them. Playfully, of course."

Sam laughs. "They beg for that? Wow, you must be super hot in bed."

Hugh grins and starts to speak.

I cut him off before he can finish one syllable. "Can we please stop talking about Hugh's sex life?"

Lord Sommerleigh smiles and slaps my arm. "Relax, mate. I'm not after your girl. Even I wouldn't stoop that low."

"Yes, I know. But your escapades aren't an appropriate topic for conversation at a backyard party."

"Fair enough. Sorry."

"No need to apologize."

Hugh checks his mobile, but he seems to be looking at the clock on its screen rather than wanting to make a call. "I should leave, anyway. My best mate needs a hand, and I promised to fly to Inverness to offer my support."

"What's wrong with Callum?"

"He injured himself again, and his brother has sent him to physical therapy in Inverness."

"Who's Callum?" Sam asks.

"Callum MacTaggart," I say. "He and Hugh have been best mates for years. Callum used to be a firefighter, but now he does carpentry work."

My wife glances at Hugh. "What kind of work do you do?"

"I am a wastrel, I'm afraid. A figurehead at my family's company. I spend most of my time getting into trouble."

He doesn't sound happy about that. Might Hugh want to settle down at last? I'll believe that on the day aliens land on the lawn of Buckingham Palace.

Well, Reese Dixon became a family man. So did Nick Hunter. If they could change their lives, maybe Hugh can too. He's a decent bloke deep down, not at all the way everyone outside of our group of friends thinks he is.

"I'd better go," Hugh says. "A desperate Scot needs me to rescue him from a harpy who wants to torture him in the name of physical therapy." He chuckles. "Though Callum has probably exaggerated how awful the bird is. He'll probably be shagging her by the time I get there."

"Have a good trip," I say. "At least you'll have a nice holiday in Scotland."

"Callum says the American Wives Club is determined to help him, whether he wants them to or not." Hugh sighs. "They'll probably try to marry me off too. Well, cheers."

He walks away, disappearing around the side of the house.

"The American Wives Club?" Sam says. "What's that about?"

"It's a sort of club started by the American wives of Lachlan, Rory, and Aidan MacTaggart. Since then, they've recruited every new MacTaggart spouse who's American. They've also expanded to create the British Branch of the American Wives Club." I wrap an arm around my wife and pull her close. "If you haven't been inducted yet, I'm sure you will be soon."

"What does this club do?"

"Meddle in other people's lives. They do it because they want to help everyone find a happy ending." I tug her even closer. "I didn't need anyone to meddle on my behalf. I literally fell into your arms."

"No, you fell into the snow. I pulled you out."

"Close enough. Let's go inside and make some noise."

She lifts her brows. "With all our friends out here?"

"Yes. Are you up for it?"

My wife smiles in the sexy way that always gets me revved up. "Absolutely. Let's do it."

We sneak away and rush upstairs to our bedroom, then we make plenty of noise. Our friends don't give a toss. They've done some wild things of their own, so nobody will complain about what Sam and I do together.

But I can't help wondering about Hugh. Does Lord Steamy want to settle down? What about Callum and the physical therapist? Not sure why, but I have a strange intuition that Hugh's holiday in Scotland might turn into something else. Hugh does have a way with women, and he often causes trouble whether he means to or not.

Not my problem. It's up to the American Wives Club to sort it out.

A few days later, when I tell Nick about Hugh and Callum, he just smiles. "Don't worry. The British Branch is mobilizing for an invasion of the Highlands."

Lord Steamy might wish he'd never gone to Scotland.

Hugh Parrish returns in *The American Wives Club* (A Hot Brits/Hot Scots/Au Naturel Crossover) and in *One Hot Scandal* (Hot Brits, Book Seven).

Anna Durand is a bestselling, multi-award-winning author of contemporary and paranormal romance. Her books have earned bestseller status on every major retailer and wonderful reviews from readers around the world. But that's the boring spiel. Here are the really cool things you want to know about Anna!

Born on Lackland Air Force Base in Texas, Anna grew up moving here, there, and everywhere thanks to her dad's job as an instructor pilot. She's lived in Texas (twice), Mississippi, California (twice), Michigan (twice), and Alaska—and now Ohio.

As for her writing, Anna has always made up stories in her head, but she didn't write them down until her teen years. Those first awful books went into the trash can a few years later, though she learned a lot from those stories. Eventually, she would pen her first romance novel, the paranormal romance *Willpower*, and she's never looked back since.

Want even more details about Anna? Get access to her extended bio when you subscribe to her newsletter and download the free bonus ebook, *Hot Scots Confidential*. You'll also get hot deleted scenes, character interviews, fun facts, and more! Plus you'll receive the short story *Tempted by a Kiss* and mutliple bonus chapters in both ebook and audiobook formats.

Visit AnnaDurand.com to sign up.